"I'll take the j[ob]"

Tucker didn't know w[hat to say?] This woman in his life, in his home. She had secrets. She had a brokenness that scared the daylights out of him.

She made his niece smile. For that matter, she made him smile.

"If you'd rather find someone else, I understand. But I could fill the spot until you find someone more suitable."

"What made you change your mind?" he asked.

Clara gave a casual lift of a shoulder. "A lot of reasons. Shay needs someone who understands what she's going through. I know how much it hurts to feel abandoned by the people who should care the most."

"Shay is a challenge," he warned.

If she worked for him, could he remain impartial, not getting involved, not caring what her story might be? He doubted it. But he had to do what Shay's parents hadn't done. He had to put his niece first, and for some reason, he thought this woman might be the right thing for Shay.

"I need a challenge." She smiled.

Brenda Minton lives in the Ozarks with her husband, children, cats, dogs and strays. She is a pastor's wife, Sunday-school teacher, coffee addict and is sleep-deprived. Not in that order. Her dream to be an author for Harlequin started somewhere in the pages of a romance novel about a young American woman stranded in a Spanish castle. Her dreams came true, and twenty-plus books later, she is an author hoping to inspire young girls to dream.

Books by Brenda Minton

Love Inspired

Her Small Town Secret
Her Christmas Dilemma

Mercy Ranch

Reunited with the Rancher
The Rancher's Christmas Match
Her Oklahoma Rancher
The Rancher's Holiday Hope
The Prodigal Cowboy
The Rancher's Holiday Arrangement

Bluebonnet Springs

Second Chance Rancher
The Rancher's Christmas Bride
The Rancher's Secret Child

Visit the Author Profile page at LoveInspired.com for more titles.

Her Christmas Dilemma

Brenda Minton

LOVE INSPIRED
INSPIRATIONAL ROMANCE

LOVE INSPIRED®
INSPIRATIONAL ROMANCE

Recycling programs
for this product may
not exist in your area.

ISBN-13: 978-1-335-75893-4

Her Christmas Dilemma

Copyright © 2021 by Brenda Minton

This edition published by arrangement with Harlequin Books S.A.

For questions and comments about the quality of this book, please contact us
at CustomerService@Harlequin.com.

Love Inspired
22 Adelaide St. West, 40th Floor
Toronto, Ontario M5H 4E3, Canada
www.LoveInspired.com

Printed in U.S.A.

Who shall separate us from the love of Christ?
shall tribulation, or distress, or persecution,
or famine, or nakedness, or peril, or sword?

As it is written,
For they sake we are killed all the day long;
we are accounted as sheep for the slaughter.

Nay, in all these things we are more than
conquerors through him that loved us.
—*Romans* 8:35–37

To all of the women who have had to make decisions that others might not understand. You are loved. God's love, His grace and His forgiveness are yours.

And to my amazing friend Lori Wech, for being willing to read at the drop of a hat.

Chapter One

The vivid colors of a Missouri sunset filtered through the dusty windows of the workshop, the beams of light picking up the glittering dust particles that danced in the air. Clara Fisher sat back on the stool where she'd been perched for several hours, after helping to clean up Thanksgiving dinner.

She'd needed a quiet place to think. Working on one of Nan's custom riverboats had been the perfect escape. The Jon boats were long, wide and flat-bottomed, perfect for skimming the waters of the James River that meandered through Pleasant, Missouri.

If not for the brisk, late November weather, Clara might have been tempted to put a boat on the river. Nothing soothed like a float trip. Maybe another day, a warmer day would come, and she'd be impulsive enough to follow through with the idea. Maybe she'd ask Nan to go.

Sitting on the stool, the sander hovering above the wood she'd been working on, fear hit the way it often did. Almost always at sunset, when darkness crept across the horizon, the anxiety would rear its ugly head.

During the daylight hours she could convince herself she was fine. Sunset revealed the lies she'd been telling herself. If she'd been just fine, she would have still been in St. Louis, living her life, achieving success in her job as a hotel manager. A person who was fine wouldn't be hiding away in Pleasant, making Jon boats and crying herself to sleep at night.

Nan Guthrie, Clara's foster mom from years earlier, certainly suspected something. But she wouldn't ask questions, not yet. She'd told Clara when she'd arrived here a month earlier that she could share when she was ready to share.

That hadn't yet happened.

Outside the shop, Nan's collie barked. It was a low, fierce sound that warned of an intruder. Or a bear. Maybe a skunk. With Sugar, a person never really knew what a bark meant.

The door creaked open on squeaky hinges.

Clara forced herself to focus on what she knew to be true, not on the fear that was grounded in memories. She was in Nan's workshop, not a parking garage near the hotel she'd managed in St. Louis.

She was in Pleasant, Missouri. She could smell the varnish of boats, the dust of sanded wood and autumn in the wind. She repeated her mantra: she was safe. The door opened wider, and the intruder peeked inside.

Not much of an intruder.

The girl who sneaked through the door obviously hadn't noticed that she wasn't alone. The teenager's focus seemed to be glued to Nan's old moped. Clara's lips tugged into a smile that surprised her and almost brought a burst of laughter. That moped had been rusted junk when Clara first came to live with Nan fifteen years earlier.

Clara cleared her throat, gaining the attention of the would-be thief. The girl jumped and then quickly shifted in Clara's direction, grabbing a nearby broom and wielding it as a weapon. Face-to-face, Clara got a better look at the girl. She stood there in her faded hoodie and ripped-up jeans, clutching the pole in a white-knuckled grip. She was in her early teens with light brown hair pulled back in a ponytail and a baseball cap on her head.

"Stay back," the girl threatened in a shaky voice.

Clara raised her hands.

"I'm just curious. Where do you think you're going, and how will that old moped get you to your destination?"

"None of your business."

"Okay. What if we start with introductions? I'm Clara," she said simply with a casual lift of one shoulder. "And you are?"

"None of your business."

"That doesn't seem fair. I told you my name."

"Haven't you realized life isn't fair?" the girl mocked.

Clara had indeed realized that. She'd known that fact for as long as she could remember. From early childhood, living in poverty with parents who never seemed to work or to think about the child they'd brought into the world, she'd known that life wasn't fair. Then one day, she'd had enough. Her mom had smacked her for eating the last frozen pizza. Her dad had chased her through the house with a fireplace tool. No one had heard. No one had cared. She'd grabbed a few things, tossed them in a backpack and climbed out her bedroom window, leaving the door locked to her parents as she ran down the road.

A police officer had found her walking, no real destination or plan, just a desire to escape. Family Services had been called, and her situation investigated. That evening her life had changed. She'd been placed with Nan Guthrie.

This girl, too, had a backpack over one shoulder, as if she was planning her own escape. But there the comparison ended. Hers was expensive-looking, not a hand-me-down or thrift-store bargain. Her shoes were also name-brand, expensive and not scuffed. Those things didn't mean she couldn't have a real reason to escape, it just meant she wasn't coming from the same type of home Clara had been running away from.

Clara's heart shuddered at the thought, at all of the many things that would make a kid want to steal an ancient moped.

"If you tell me what's going on, I could get you some help."

"I don't need help. I just need to go." The girl edged toward the moped but not before Clara saw the tear that trickled down her cheek.

"It doesn't work," Clara offered. "I ran away once. I had to get away from my parents."

"Were they mean?" the girl asked, curiosity getting the better of her.

"They were a lot of things," Clara said as the memories ran through her mind like old movie clips, snippets of the pain, the fear that the people who'd given her life had caused. "I could help you. Everyone needs a friend who understands."

The roar of a car approaching the shop stopped their conversation. Clara shot the girl a questioning look.

"Great. Thanks to you, he's found me, and he's going to make me go back."

"Back to what?" Clara asked.

Before the girl could answer, the door flew open, and there he was, a mountain of a man with the same brown hair as the runaway. Except he was tall, very tall. His shoulders were broad. A frown tugged at the corners of his mouth.

Unfortunately, Clara couldn't scold. She couldn't speak. She couldn't breathe. Her vision narrowed, and she had to force air into her lungs. Memories, only a few months old and still vivid, overwhelmed the present.

She couldn't let that happen.

This man, this stranger, wasn't her attacker. His focus wasn't on her, it was on the girl who had quickly shed her courage and moved to Clara's side. She gave Clara a curious look as she grabbed the boat paddle and shoved it into Clara's hands.

"You have to protect me. He's going to try and take me back with him. I can't go with him. I want to go to my mom." The teen sobbed, and something about that sound jolted Clara back to the situation at hand.

Now tethered to the present, Clara said, "She isn't going anywhere with you."

Humor flickered in his hazel eyes. He was amused. She started to tell him there was nothing funny about this situation, but even Clara could see that, from the stranger's point of view, maybe it was laughable. She was standing in front of him with a boat paddle as her only defense.

It didn't help that the teen jumped forward and yelled, "You're not taking me alive."

Clara shot the girl a look. "That's a little dramatic, don't you think?"

"Well, you're not doing anything to help." The girl grabbed the boat paddle and brandished it as if it was a sword.

The man had taken a few steps in their direction, strolling as if he hadn't a care in the world. He was more than a foot taller than Clara's five-foot-nothing inches. The closer he got, the more cornered she felt. Her amusement seeped away, and so did her courage. There was a back door to the workshop, but Nan's ancient pickup that she planned to restore was blocking the escape route.

"I think you should leave," Clara managed as she met hazel eyes that now flickered with concern.

"I don't think I can. That's my niece, and she has to go with me." He hesitated as he studied her face. "Are you okay?"

"I'm fine," she insisted. "Just back up, and we'll discuss this."

She really needed him to give her space.

With a flick of his index finger, he pushed his cowboy hat back, probably to get a better look at them. She hated all of that cool, cowboy calm, especially when her skin had gone clammy.

"There's nothing to discuss," he informed her. "You're interfering in something that doesn't concern you."

"You need to leave, or I'll call the police." Clara reached for her phone.

"I'll save you the trouble," the man said with a drawl.

"Since that's a sander you're reaching for, I'll call them myself. Shay, you're coming home with me."

The sander? She drew her hand back, because he was right. Her phone was in her pocket, not on the table. The girl giggled.

She was no longer *the girl*. She had a name: *Shay*. The giant was her uncle.

"You can't let him take me," Shay whispered. "I just want to go home."

"You know you can't go home," he answered, and his tone had softened, taking on a note of sympathy. "Your mom is out of state, and your dad is out of the country."

"I know," she mumbled. "And neither of them want me."

"That isn't true, Shay," he said, seeming truly sorry.

Clara was on the wrong side of the argument. She didn't want to be on his side. Not when he made her feel a strange combination of unease, panic and attraction.

The attraction made no sense. She wouldn't, couldn't feel that, not in her present situation. She was too focused on making it through each day and finding answers to even think of a man as attractive.

Sidetracked by her own thoughts, Clara was slow to react when Shay sprinted for the moped. The giant went after her, and Sugar ran in circles, barking. The door opened, and Nan Guthrie joined the melee.

Clara sank to the stool and watched as Nan took control of the situation.

Tucker Church looked from the woman who had previously been Shay's defender to his niece who seemed to be making a last-ditch attempt to escape. He was torn between helping the woman, who now sat pale and shaken, to stopping Shay. Not that his niece would get anywhere on the ancient moped.

Still, duty prevailed. He grabbed his niece and pulled her off the bike.

Shay smacked at him, the gesture resembling a pesky fly more than it did abuse. He tossed her over his shoulder, turning to face Nan as she warned them all to calm down.

"Sorry, Nan. I didn't mean to bring this trouble to your doorstep. Unfortunately, Shay had other plans."

"I'm going home to Jefferson City," Shay yelled as she beat his back with her fists. "Let me down. Just let me go. You don't want me any more than they do."

She could hit him all day and it wouldn't leave a mark, but the words hurt his heart. She shouldn't feel that way, as if no one wanted her. He made eye contact with the woman who'd been doing her best to protect Shay. She remained seated, blond curls framing her pale face. Dark brown eyes reflected the horror he felt after hearing his niece's words.

He set Shay back on her feet but kept hold of her arm. "I do want you, Shay. I know you think your parents don't, but they do. They just…"

He didn't know what to say, how to end the statement in order to convince his niece that her parents cared.

Shay's hazel eyes overflowed with tears that she dashed away. "They're selfish. That's what I heard you tell my mom last week when she called."

He blanched. "You shouldn't be listening in on private conversations. What I said to my sister—"

"—is true," Nan Guthrie piped up in her characteristic I'm-seventy-can-say-what-I-want way. When he gave her a look, she shrugged. "Let's be honest, Tucker.

Your sister is being selfish. Her daughter knows it. You know it. We all know it. But that's neither here nor there. The problem you seem to have is convincing your niece to stay here because you want her. She also has to see sense and understand she can't go traipsing around the country on a moped that's nothing but scrap metal and rust. It's November, girl. You're smarter than that."

"I just thought my mom would be here for Christmas."

"She'll be here for Christmas," Tucker assured his niece. "If I have to go to the state capitol and drag her back to Pleasant myself, she'll be here. Meanwhile we have to find a new housekeeper."

"I'm not sure why we need a housekeeper," Shay murmured.

"We need a housekeeper because I can't run a business, a farm and a home plus chase you down every other—" He suddenly remembered they had an audience. "We can talk about this at home."

"Maybe we have a solution to your housekeeper problem." Nan beamed.

He was afraid to ask. "And what would that be?"

Other than his parents coming home from the mission trip to Mexico. He'd been telling them for the past few months that they didn't have to leave their post. He was starting to doubt that now.

Nan, spritely at seventy with short silvery hair and a penchant for wearing her rubber farm boots everywhere, grinned big and inclined her head toward the other woman.

"Clara needs a job," she said, as if this solved all of the world's problems.

The woman came to her feet, and he couldn't help

but notice that, not only was she pretty she was scared silly. Of him? Of Shay? He wasn't quite sure.

"I don't think so," she shot back at Nan. "I'm quite happy helping you."

"You need something to do," Nan insisted. "Something other than building boats with me."

"She doesn't want the job." Tucker winked at the woman and watched as her cheeks turned rosy.

Flirting was an art he'd learned late in life, and he still wasn't too accomplished at it. He'd never been a ladies' man.

The one standing under the bright florescent lighting looked like a woman who could make him lose his common sense. She already had him winking. Winking was not usually part of his flirting tactics.

"No, I really don't," she answered. "I'm only here temporarily."

Should he feel relieved or let down?

He studied the face of the woman Nan had called Clara. Did he know her? He guessed if she'd lived at Nan's, the odds were good that they'd met.

"You should introduce us," he told Nan, his gaze traveling again to the woman at her side.

"I guess I assumed the two of you had met," Nan said. "Tucker Church, I'd like you to meet Clara Fisher. She's one of my kids."

One of Nan's foster daughters. She'd had a dozen or more over the years. Tucker had known a few, but this one, a few years younger than himself, didn't look familiar.

He walked across the room so that he could greet Clara Fisher properly. He held a hand out while still holding on to his niece.

"Clara, nice to meet you."

Clara looked from his outstretched hand to his face. It was a long moment before she held her hand out, sliding warm fingers into his. Her grip was strong but fleeting. When he released her hand, she stepped back, putting space between them.

"Nice to meet you, too. But I'm afraid I'm not interested in a job." She gave his niece a genuine smile, then her gaze lifted to meet his. "I think that we probably met in school, but you were a senior and I was new to Pleasant and just a freshman."

He couldn't imagine forgetting Clara Fisher, with her dark brown eyes that held secrets and a smile that was soft and captivating. He found himself wishing he could make her smile again.

The thought was one that couldn't be dwelt on, not when Shay stood next to him, elbowing him with a surprisingly sharp jab.

"What?" he asked more harshly than he'd intended.

"She doesn't want the job," Shay whispered. "Can we go home now?"

Go home? Was this the same kid who had just tried to leave town on a moped?

"Of course she doesn't want to work for me." He gave his niece a warning look. "She's probably heard the stories about you running off two housekeepers."

"Then, isn't it better if we don't have a housekeeper?" Shay said gloomily. When had she become so gloomy? As a little girl she'd been all smiles and giggles. What had changed?

Oh, right, as her parents' relationship had fallen apart, their daughter had suffered.

He sighed and gave the woman, Clara, a pleading look.

"Would you take my number? In case you change your mind about the position?"

"I won't change my mind," she insisted.

"Of course." He had no right to feel disappointed. She was a stranger. She probably had a real career. And yet, he was disappointed.

It was for the best, he told himself.

He knew better than to get tangled up with one of Nan's girls, even the adult ones. In high school he'd dated one of her foster daughters. She'd broken his heart in a thousand different ways. Clara had the same haunted look as Junie. He sighed, remembering. Junie had been too much reality for a boy who hadn't experienced real hurt.

"Well, we should go so that the two of you can get back to your work," he said as he kept hold of Shay's arm, walking her toward the door.

"That was close," Shay said, almost under her breath.

"What?" He couldn't have heard her correctly.

"Nothing. I just think you almost made a mistake trying to hire her. I bet she can't even clean."

He didn't disagree with his niece. But it wasn't the cleaning he was worried about.

Clara looked like a woman who had been broken and was trying to put herself back together. When he replaced Mrs. Jenkins, he needed someone strong, someone who could stand up to Shay.

The woman who replaced Mrs. Jenkins couldn't have soulful brown eyes and a smile that made him want to take chances.

Chapter Two

Three days later, Clara found herself in the passenger seat of Nan's boat of a sedan. The four-door car had cracked leather seats, an ancient radio that had to be tuned by a knob and fake wood paneling on the doors.

"'Go to church with me,'" Clara said in a monotone voice as she hunkered down in the front seat. "'It'll be fun,' she said."

She didn't have anything against church or against God. It was the car, the people…everything.

She just didn't want to feel all the feels that would hit her when she walked through the doors of Pleasant Community Church. Especially today, the Sunday after Thanksgiving. Potluck Sunday. Visitor Sunday. Crowded and Overwhelming Sunday.

Nan finished backing into a parking space, and then she confronted Clara with a hard stare. "For a minute I thought the old you had returned."

"The old me?" Clara said, feeling shocked. She didn't know if she remembered the old Clara.

"Yes, the old you. I saw a hint of her last night. The

old Clara was tough as nails, and she had a quick wit hiding beneath all of that teen angst. She was a survivor."

"I'm surviving," Clara assured her foster mom. She didn't like the flicker of worry in Nan's eyes. She would never want to hurt or worry the older woman.

"I want you to do more than survive." Nan's focus moved to the church, a simple white building with a bell tower. An addition at the back housed a fellowship hall and classrooms. A separate building was used for youth services and community activities.

"Nay, in all these things we are more than conquerors through Him that loved us," Clara repeated the verse from Romans that hung on the dining-room wall of Nan's old farmhouse. The needlepoint wall hanging had been added to by each and every girl that ever lived at Nan's. It was a hodgepodge of names, crosses, stars, hearts and more.

"I'm glad you remember," Nan said softly. "You've always been a conqueror. Whatever happened to you, and I do wish you'd talk about it, you're going to survive."

"Will I?" Clara asked. She truly wanted affirmation of that. There were days when she believed, but there were also moments when she thought she'd always be lost in the fear.

"You will find your joy again, Clara. That was something about you that I always admired. From the moment you came through my door, a scrappy teenager with chopped-off hair and a chip on your shoulder, you were funny. You tried to find things to laugh about."

"Defense mechanism," Clara quipped.

"Maybe a little. But I always thought the two of us

were kindred spirits. We could go through the hard times but still find the laughter that made us strong."

"Oh, Nan, I wish I was more like you."

"You're more like me than you know. Hiding your secrets and trying to work it all out on your own."

"What are you hiding, Nan?"

Nan's expression clouded. "I'm not hiding anything these days. If I hide it, I might not find it."

Nan had the beginning stages of dementia. The diagnosis changied all of their lives, and their futures. She'd informed the doctor that he hadn't written the story of her life, her God had, and she'd let Him handle this. But the truth was, Nan was frightened. Clara should have seen it sooner.

"We'll make it through this together."

Nan reached for her hand, clasping it in a cool but strong grip. "I know we will. And eventually, you're going to talk to me."

"Eventually," she agreed. When she felt as if she could talk without falling apart.

They walked through the doors of the church together, arm in arm, holding each other close. Clara thought that Nan did it for her sake, but maybe Nan needed it, too.

The congregation still milled about, greeting one another, discussing life, cattle prices and the lack of rain. Rain was always a topic of conversation in a farm town. Either they were getting too much, not as much as their neighbor or none at all.

Clara breathed a sigh of relief when they slid into a pew with Nan's other foster daughter, Avery, her daughter Quinn and her new husband, Grayson Stone.

"Hey, look who decided to join us." Avery wrapped

an arm around Clara's shoulder and gave her a light squeeze. "I'm glad you're here."

"I'd like to say the same," Clara said. "The jury is out."

Avery, an RN, gave her a look that was half concerned foster sister and half medical professional. Her eyes narrowed as she studied Clara.

"Deep breaths," Avery whispered.

"Right, breathing. It should be an easy thing. Inhale, exhale. But if it is such a natural process, why does it feel like there's an elephant on my chest?"

"I wish I knew, but since you won't talk…" Avery gave her another meaningful look. She didn't know what to tell her.

It was hard enough that the memories crashed into every situation without invitation, but to put it into words, to talk about it, that would be so difficult. It would make it real. Again.

If she could bury the memory forever, she would. The parking garage. The darkness. The man with the ski mask on his face. The barrel of the gun. She closed her eyes, wishing it all away. Praying it away. *More than conquerors through Christ who strengthens*, she repeated in her mind over and over until the fear subsided, until she could breathe again.

The music had started. The hymn was old and familiar, timeless the way hymns should be. The second song was a contemporary one. The next a Christmas song.

She loved Christmas. She loved the music, the decorations, the story of God's plan of salvation through a child. Her throat constricted, and she blinked back tears.

"I'll be right back," she whispered.

"I can go with—" Avery started.

"No, I'm good. I just need a drink of water." And a place where she didn't feel trapped.

She hurried from the sanctuary, through a side door. A moment later she entered the blessed silence of the brightly lit fellowship hall with its tile floors, white walls and bright fluorescent lights. She breathed in deep, felt the elephant lighten its weight on her lungs. She should name him, since he seemed to be a big part of her life these days. Clyde the Elephant. If she named him, maybe he wouldn't have such control over her emotions. Maybe if Clyde was a fluffy elephant with kind eyes?

The fact that she was naming her anxiety meant she must truly be losing it.

She leaned against the wall, just for a moment. She closed her eyes and continued to breathe, to relax, to find peace. She prayed, because praying meant giving the fear to Someone bigger than herself. Footsteps echoed in the far corner of the room. Her eyes jerked open.

He stood in the doorway of the kitchen, tall and broad across the shoulders, his sable hair a little unruly, dark-framed glasses on his straight nose. How did Tucker look bookish and tough at the same time?

Suddenly, her focus was stolen by the need to rush to the large garbage can by the door. She leaned over, too sick to be embarrassed.

"Are you okay?" he asked, his hand on her back.

She needed for him to not touch her. "I'm okay." She raised a hand to push him away. "But please, give me a minute."

"Of course. I'll go get you a glass of water."

She nodded, her head still in the trash can.

He returned, handing her a damp paper towel and the glass. She wiped her face.

"Thank you," she said, avoiding looking at him as she raised the water to her lips.

"No worries. Can I get you anything else? Do you need Nan? Or Avery?"

"No, I'm good. Really. It was just the excitement of being back in church, combined with the strange egg thing Nan made for breakfast." She attempted a bright smile as she maneuvered around him. He moved with her, his expression still filled with concern and sympathy.

"I'm good," she repeated. "You can go back to doing whatever you were doing."

If he walked away, she would be able to relax. But it would be rude to tell him to go so she could breathe.

"Basting turkeys," he said. She must have looked as confused as he felt because he arched a brow. "They're on the smoker outside. The turkeys for our lunch. That's what I'm doing."

"Oh. So you cook?"

"I'm thirty-two and single. Of course I cook. If I didn't, I'd starve."

"And your niece," she said, then paused to see if he would walk away. She wanted, needed for him to walk away. She needed to not feel as if she wanted him to stay and talk to her. A man. A stranger.

It made sense that she should want him to go. The part where she wanted him to stay, that was not at all logical. So of course she took a seat at one of the round tables, decorated for the holidays.

Without invitation, he sat next to her, leaving a couple of chairs between them. She appreciated that.

"My niece is glad that I can cook, but she'd rather eat at Tilly's Café every night of the week," he said in a dry tone but with humor flickering in his hazel eyes. "And I don't really have the time to do a lot of meal planning, let alone cooking."

"I don't blame her. I always loved Tilly's chicken fried steak."

"It's the best," he agreed.

She took another sip of water, and her stomach began to settle. "Did you find a new housekeeper?"

"Not yet. I put an ad in the paper, but there are few locals willing to take on a job that requires them to chase after Shay. Her reputation precedes her."

"I think she's sweet, just afraid."

"Afraid?" He looked puzzled.

"She's afraid her parents don't want her back. Maybe she's afraid you feel stuck with her. How long has she been with you?"

"About a year."

"Do they visit?" she asked. "I'm sorry, it isn't my business." She just wanted to talk about something other than herself. Focusing on Tucker and his niece released some of the tension that had been building inside her.

"Not enough. I wish I could say they weren't selfish. But they are. They've forgotten that a marriage with children means it isn't all about them. They want what they want, and neither of them is thinking about their daughter."

"What has she done? I mean, other than trying to steal a moped?" she asked.

"Nothing terrible," he answered. "She pulled a few capers in Jefferson City. Since she's been here, she's skipped school. She'd pulled a few pranks on teachers. She might have taped some super good firecracker poppers on the sole of the last housekeeper's shoes. She put her shoes on, took a step, and it sounded like fireworks going off."

"Oh my," Clara said, holding back a smile. "That is bad."

"Yes, and it makes it difficult to run a business. Fortunately, winter means I have a little bit of a break."

"I can imagine," she said with genuine sympathy.

"I need to check the turkeys again," he said as he looked at his watch. "Are you sure you don't want the job?"

"Checking turkeys?" she teased. "No, thanks, I'm not much of a cook."

"Funny." He winked, the gesture taking her by surprise.

He didn't seem like the winking type. In the black wire-frame glasses, he seemed nerdy and boring and, yet, he wasn't. Tucker was ruggedly handsome. A big man with broad shoulders. He was kind and thoughtful. Maybe even insightful. He was the type of man she should avoid. Because it would be too easy to like him. Because he had his own troubles, and he didn't need to be saddled with hers. And he was probably the type who felt naturally compelled to help others.

"I appreciate the humor, but I meant the housekeeper job," he said. He was determined, she realized. Or desperate.

"No, I think not. I don't know how long I'll be in the area. I'm on leave from my job, but in the next couple of months I have to make a decision about where I'm going."

She had several big decisions to make. The thought caused another wave of nausea.

"What is it that you do?"

"Hotel management. I work for a big chain, and I might be taking a job out of the country."

"I see. I guess that would make it hard for you to be a housekeeper and nanny."

She smiled at him. "Exactly. I'm hoping that by spring I'll be living on the coast of Mexico."

"Then I can't say that I blame you for turning down a job as a housekeeper in Pleasant, Missouri." He was moving from his seat, away from her.

"Thank you," she said as he started to walk away. "For rescuing me."

He tipped an imaginary hat. "It's been a pleasure, ma'am."

Once upon a time she would have flirted with him, maybe even asked him out for coffee. But that Clara no longer existed. She'd disappeared in a parking garage, along with her courage and her strength. Now she was someone different, someone less trusting, someone afraid of shadows, dark places and the future. She wasn't someone that a man like Tucker Church should waste his dimpled smiles and flirty winks on.

She was hollow inside. Hollow, except for one very small thing. That even now was making a huge impact on her life. What would she do in six months when it arrived, and she had to look at it and see the face of the man who had attacked her?

She closed her eyes and imagined the face of Tucker Church, the way he'd looked when he winked at her. If she was a different person, she would have opened herself up to possibilities.

* * *

Tucker escaped. He didn't like being a coward, but there was something about Clara Fisher. Something soft, something attractive and something broken. He figured that *something* about her could break a man's heart, and Tucker was all about preserving his. Someday he would meet the right woman. Right woman, right time. He didn't want his heart all used up when that day happened.

Time worried him. He wasn't getting any younger.

Out the back door he went, to the smokers where the turkeys had been cooking for quite some time. The aroma filled the cool autumn air. The leaves had fallen, and the trees were bare. It was the holiday season, and something about that gave a man hope.

He hoped he and Shay would survive this season of their lives, with him trying to figure out how to parent a teenager with all the typical teen problems, plus the ones her parents had added on—just to make her life a little more difficult. Christmas was just under a month away. They needed to decorate a tree, do a little shopping and help prepare Pleasant for the first annual Christmas Crafters Fair.

They were even setting up a small ice-skating rink at his campground. The place would be empty until spring, so why not find a use for it? Christmas seemed the perfect time to set up the rink, string some lights and make it an affordable place for families to spend quality time together. He'd even found a vendor to sell hot chocolate, cider and coffee.

He had a lot to do in the next month, and that ought to keep his mind from being distracted. Except an unwelcome thought slipped into his mind. The pale face of Clara Fisher as she leaned over the garbage can. Not exactly romantic, but an image that might haunt his thoughts for a day or two.

"How's them turkeys coming along?" Jack, an old timer who'd been coming to Pleasant Community Church for as long as Tucker could remember, joined him.

Jack had dressed for the special occasion. He'd donned a button-up shirt and a bow tie with his usual overalls.

"I think they're done," Tucker assured him. Jack leaned in to take a look.

"I think you're right. I'll have the men get them inside and carved up. You did good work, Tucker."

"Thanks, Jack." Tucker closed the lid on the smoker. "I guess the service is over?"

"Almost. The prep crew is getting everything out of the fridge." Jack hooked a thumb through the strap of his denim bib overalls. "When I came in, one of Nan's girls was in there crying."

Tucker didn't want to hear that but couldn't ignore it. Jack was eyeing him, as if he thought Tucker had done something to her. Or maybe he thought Tucker should help her out.

"I think she's having a bad morning," Tucker informed the older gentleman. "If she's still in there, I can get Nan or Avery."

"Nan found her. I just wondered if there's anything we can do to help."

"Not that I know of."

"That's a right shame," Jack said with a shake of his head.

"Yes, it is," Tucker agreed. "I'm sure Nan will take care of her."

Jack gave him a passing look, the kind that asked why he'd turned coldhearted. He wasn't; he just knew better than to step too far into someone else's problems.

"Well, I'll see to getting the turkeys inside," Jack said.

Fifteen minutes later they were putting the first of the turkeys on trays next to the ham. Pastor Wilson had asked a blessing on the food, and the line was beginning to form. With his job now completed, Tucker went in search of Shay. He found her sitting off by herself. He wasn't the only one who had spotted the lone teen. Clara started across the room in her direction. She spotted Tucker, hesitated, but then joined them.

"I'm not hungry," Shay said, not making eye contact with either of them.

"You didn't eat breakfast," Tucker responded.

"Is there a law that says I have to be hungry?" Shay countered.

Tucker didn't know how to respond to that question. Should he correct her attitude? Maybe he should mention the cell phone she always had in her hand and how it could be taken away.

"Sometimes I don't feel hungry, either, but if I put food on my plate, I find that my appetite returns." Clara sat down next to his niece, giving him a quick look as she did. A look that asked permission, he thought.

He gave a slight nod, confirming his approval. Call him a chicken, but a teen girl was a lot to deal with, and he was man enough to admit that he didn't have all the required skills.

"I don't like holidays," Shay told Clara. "I mean, it

isn't his fault," she said, barely giving him a look. "It just doesn't feel like a holiday."

"I totally get that," Clara commiserated. "We have a choice, Shay. We can sit back here by ourselves, or we can get in line and conquer the potluck by picking everything that is bad for us. Why don't we start by eating dessert first?"

Shay grinned at the suggestion. "I do love pecan pie."

"I love Nan's stuffing even more than dessert," Clara said as she held her plate out to the lady serving from the big pan. "But I'm also going to make sure I get a piece of cheesecake!"

"I see that I'm no longer needed here," Tucker said as the two continued to talk. He couldn't be upset, not when Shay was smiling and being half-agreeable.

And not with Clara. Not with someone who clearly had to step outside her comfort zone in order to reach his niece. Clara looked up at him with chocolate-brown eyes and a hint of a smile.

"You can go through the line with us," Shay offered to Tucker. "It'll make you less conspicuous if you're in a group and not towering over everyone in church like Goliath."

"Thanks," he said, gesturing for them to go ahead of him. He would follow, lurking over them like Goliath and wishing he'd taken his opportunity and escaped.

They were standing in line surrounded when Clara turned to face him. Her brown eyes sought his with a seriousness that didn't surprise him. She was a strange mixture of serious and funny, with a whole lot of sad thrown in.

"I'll take the job," she said, as if they'd been discussing the job.

"I'm sorry?"

"Have you hired someone?" She glanced at her watch. "In the past fifteen minutes?"

"No, I haven't. I…" He didn't know what to say. This woman had secrets. She had a brokenness that scared the daylights out of him.

But she made his niece smile. For that matter, she made him smile.

"If you'd rather find someone else, I understand. I'm obviously not experienced. I've already admitted that I can't cook and I'm also only here temporarily, but I could fill the spot until you find someone more suitable."

"What made you change your mind?" he asked, glad that his niece had wandered ahead to talk to a friend.

She shrugged a shoulder and glanced around. "A lot of reasons. Shay needs someone who understands what she's going through. I do know how much it hurts to feel abandoned by the people who should care the most. Also, I feel the need to do more than sit by myself in Nan's boat shop. Plus, Nan fired me this morning."

"She fired you?" He couldn't help but chuckle.

"Yeah, she did." Her eyes briefly twinkled. "She said I'm in her way. She likes her solitary time. She doesn't mind my help, but she doesn't want me to become a fixture in her shop."

"Shay is a challenge," he warned.

If she worked for him, could he remain impartial, not getting involved, not caring what her story might be? He doubted it. But he had to do what Shay's parents hadn't done: he had to put his niece first. For some reason, he thought this woman might be the right thing for Shay. For the time being.

"I need a challenge." She smiled.

"I get weekly calls from the school. I think she thinks if she's bad enough, her parents will ride to the rescue. They won't."

"I'm sorry about that. Parents aren't always what we need them to be. Sometimes they can't be, sometimes they choose not to be."

It made him angry to think about his sister and brother-in-law, the choices they'd made putting them first and Shay last. Could this woman put Shay first? "She needs people who will support her but not allow her to get away with the trouble she's causing."

"I can be that person," she assured him with a subtle lift of her chin. "Give me a week. If it doesn't work out, I'll go back to boats."

He grinned. "I guess we can give it a one-week trial. Can you be at the house tomorrow at six?"

"So early?"

"Second thoughts?" he asked.

"Only for a moment," she admitted. Then they were next in line to get plates, so they spoke no more on the subject.

Tucker was generally an optimistic person, but he knew that letting Clara into his home—and his life— was going to bring an array of problems.

First and foremost, he liked her. He liked her a lot. And that was a big problem.

Chapter Three

Clara had a lot of second thoughts about working for Tucker. Second, third, fourth and probably tenth thoughts, too, as she followed the GPS directions to Tucker's farm on Monday morning. Church's Cattle Company was a big spread that covered hundreds of acres, some of which was riverfront property.

Home.

That was the feeling she had as she drove down the narrow road to the house at the end of the lane. The house was a long brick structure with a covered front porch, where a dog lay sprawled out. He was a massive brown creature who didn't seem at all interested in her arrival.

This was the type of place that families passed down from generation to generation. It was land, a heritage, a future, as well as a connection to the past. She'd never had a home like this. What she'd had was a ramshackle house with holes in the walls and not much of a future until Nan took her in.

Until a couple of months ago, she'd rented an apartment in St. Louis, but it had never felt like home. She'd hung pictures on the walls, bought stiff, new furniture and spent most of her time there alone.

But enough travels down memory lane. She needed to be present right now, in the life she was living.

She parked and started to get out of her car. Her stomach churned, and she sat back down, waiting for the nausea to subside. For a moment she closed her eyes and breathed, her hand slowly moving to her belly. Soon it would be obvious: she wouldn't be able to hide her pregnancy.

Soon she would have to make a decision concerning the future of the child she carried. A child who might look like the man who had attacked her. How would she hold this baby, look into its eyes, name it, care for it?

More than conquerors, she told herself. *More than*.

But being a conqueror didn't solve her dilemma; it didn't give her answers.

She got out of her car but then hesitated when the mastiff clambered to his feet and growled. He took a few steps and stopped at the edge of the porch.

"Hey, buddy," she said in a friendly voice. He growled as he edged closer to the steps. The front door opened, and Tucker stepped out to rescue her.

"Dudley, down."

Dudley? The name made her smile.

"Good morning," she called out. "Is he going to eat me?"

"Humans aren't his favorite meal. Talk to him, scratch his ears, and he'll be your best friend." Tucker put his hand on the dog's head.

She approached slowly, hesitant. She'd never been a fan of dogs.

"Let him sniff your hand," Tucker encouraged.

"Don't worry, he might lick you to death, but he isn't going to hurt you."

"Famous last words," she muttered as she held her hand out to the dog. The animal peered up at her, his brown eyes large, soft, gentle. He snorted a little and nuzzled her hand. He didn't lick. She appreciated that small concession. "Hi there, Brutus."

The dog wagged his tail, thumping it against the concrete porch.

"His name is Dudley," Tucker reminded her.

"Yes, Dudley. But Brutus seems more fitting."

Tucker laughed, the sound rumbling through her like an avalanche. "Get to know him, and you'll understand why he's Dudley. He always tries to do the right thing, while tripping over his feet and making a big mess."

"I'm sure we'll get along just fine," she said, then she reached to pat the dog's head.

She looked up and found Tucker watching her, his expression somehow sweet and his hazel eyes more gray than brown. Gray like the sky and the plaid of his flannel jacket. It took her by surprise, that she noticed, and that she wanted to stand there for a moment, talking to him, listening to his low, rumbling laughter.

She had friends, and in her own way, she had family. She didn't need this man or his friendship and yet, she found the idea tempting.

There was something about Tucker that indicated he'd be a good friend to have. She didn't want to compare him to his dog, but they seemed similar. Both protective. Loyal.

"We should go inside. I'm supposed to be at the river this morning and move cattle today. The sooner we get this day started, the better."

"I hope you don't require my help for that job," she teased.

"Does that mean you're not interested?"

When his cheeks turned red, she wondered what about the statement had embarrassed him. She found it cute. He was tall, rugged and obviously confident. Men like Tucker didn't get embarrassed, or so she'd always thought.

Suddenly, a wave of the unpredictable nausea hit. Her expression must have shown her distress because his hand clasped her arm.

"Are you okay?"

She shook her head. She couldn't get the words out, and she couldn't look at him. She didn't want to see the questions or, worse, the sympathy in his eyes. He didn't wait for her reply. Still holding her arm, he led her inside and down the hall.

"There are disposable cups and washcloths in the cabinet." He then closed the door and left her alone in a small bathroom.

Clara leaned against the wall, forcing the nausea away as tears streamed down from her closed eyes. Anxiety crept up on her, colliding with the nausea, making it difficult to breathe. She slid to the cold tile floor and waited for the morning sickness to pass. Then she waited a little longer because she didn't want to face him. He was a smart man, and he would know the signs, even if she'd been able to hide them from others. He would know.

Why? The question she'd asked herself so many times in the past few months. Why hadn't she been more careful? Why hadn't she accepted the offer of the security guard to walk her to her car that night? She hadn't wanted to bother him, and she'd believed she could take care of herself.

More questions swirled around in her head. Why had God allowed this to happen to her? She'd worked so hard to become the best person she could be. At being someone other than the person her mother had created, someone who would follow the path of dysfunction and addiction. She'd told herself long ago that she didn't have to be that person. Her mother and her DNA were not the author of her story. She was. God was.

Just then, she heard a soft knock on the door, and a moment later a muffled inquiry. "Clara?"

"I'm fine." She wasn't, but she had to believe she would be.

"Do you need anything?"

She laughed at that, the sound without mirth. "I'm coming out."

She'd somehow face his interrogation, his questions. After all, he'd hired her to care for his niece. He'd want to know what was going on.

She found the facecloths in the cabinet, cleaned her face, then filled a paper cup with cold water from the sink. A moment later she opened the door to find he'd left her alone. She went in search of her new employer. He would either keep her on as housekeeper or ask her to leave. She wanted to stay. She didn't want to walk away from this job. She could tell herself that it was because she didn't like to give up, but the truth was that she genuinely liked Shay. Tucker wasn't too bad, either.

What would it hurt to like them? To give them a few short weeks of her life? The truth was, she knew it would hurt, because she could easily get attached to Shay and to Tucker.

But right now, it was best not to get attached to anyone.

Tucker felt it would be better to give her some space and privacy. He also needed a moment to wrap his mind around what was becoming more and more obvious. He'd always been pretty decent at math, but it had never taken him this long to put two and two together.

From the kitchen he could hear the soft steps as she approached. At one point it seemed as if she paused. He wondered if she was considering making a hasty retreat.

"I'm in the kitchen," he called out to her.

He knew things were about to get awkward. She entered the kitchen, and he glanced up, pushing the button to start a pot of coffee. He needed to be on the road in the next thirty minutes. It was Monday, and Shay needed a ride to school. Fortunately, he'd already made a list of things that his new housekeeper would need to accomplish today. If she stayed.

Did he want her to stay? Considering he already had a bushelful of his own problems to deal with, did he need hers, too?

"I'm sorry," she said as she came near, her gaze downcast.

He studied her and the fall of blond hair that framed her face that she now used to hide her expression. He saw the stoop of slim shoulders and then noticed what he hadn't before. The rounded belly.

He didn't know what to say.

She sighed and moved to the stove, as if preparing to cook something. "I can leave…"

He was silent for a long while, then finally found the right words. "I need a housekeeper and someone to help with Shay."

She nodded, still eyeing the gas stove. She turned a knob, and a flame circled the front burner. She quickly turned it off and glanced up. "I also can't cook. If you're looking for another reason to let me go, that's a good one."

"I'm not looking for a reason to let you go. I'm just trying to figure out my next step."

"I understand. I've been working on that myself." Her brown eyes glistened with unshed tears. "If it helps, I'm capable of learning to cook, and I can clean and do laundry."

He brushed a hand through his hair and sighed. She avoided eye contact.

"I'm not sure what to do," he said. "We can talk later."

"I'll make sure Shay eats, and I'll get her to school. It's the least I can do for you."

"Right, okay." His gaze dropped to her belly.

She crossed her arms in front of her, protectively. A long moment of silence hung between them. He had lots of questions. Like how her pregnancy and the frightened look in her eyes were connected. It didn't seem as if this was a joyous occasion for her.

Maybe the father didn't want to be in the picture? Maybe they'd broken up? He shook his head. None of his business, he reminded himself.

"I'll call you later," he said as he grabbed his cowboy hat off a hook by the door and headed for the garage.

"Okay." Her weak reply followed him to the door.

Two hours later, cool air, hard riding and cattle that weren't too cooperative hadn't improved his mood the way he'd hoped. As he pulled into the parking lot of Church's Riverside Campground and Outfitters, his thoughts were scattering in all directions. He parked near the office and sat in his truck with the window down to let cold, fresh November air in.

The campground was empty this time of year. Most tourists avoided the Ozarks in the cold winter months. The canoes, kayaks and rafts were stored in a metal building on his farm. The office on wheels remained because they would need it for the ice rink. If heavy rains threatened, he could use his truck to pull the building to higher ground.

The cabins he'd built were situated up the hill from the tent and RV camping area. It would take what was typically called a *hundred-year flood* to reach the cabins. Nevertheless, they were on stilts to keep them safe and out of water.

A truck pulled up next to his. He got out to greet his business partner, Grayson Stone. As teens the two of them used to talk about a business like this one. Tucker had started the business on a piece of land his uncle had given him.

Grayson contributed by being a building contractor and a good businessman. He'd suggested they expand. There would be a new shop with more souvenirs, clothing, food and tackle for fishing. The skating rink had also been Grayson's idea.

"What's got you sullen like a bloodhound that can't hunt?" Grayson asked as they met at the front of their trucks.

"Nothing," Tucker hedged, hoping Grayson would let it go.

"My right foot." Grayson pulled a pack of gum out of his pocket. "Gum?"

"No, thanks." He didn't know what to say. It wasn't his place to share secrets Clara might be trying to hide from her family.

"How's Clara working out for you?" Grayson asked, as if he knew where Tucker's thoughts had gone.

"She just started this morning, so it isn't like there's much to tell."

Grayson smirked. "That bad?"

"She can't cook."

Grayson chuckled. "That's a problem if you're needing a cook."

"It was the plan," he said.

Tucker headed for the rink. Grayson joined him. The workers waved but continued to work.

"Mike will be here in five minutes to talk about the glamping tents," Grayson said. "If you need to talk, now is the time."

"I don't need to talk."

Grayson shifted, pushing his dark brimmed hat up as he looked out over the river. A pale gray crane stood at the edge of the water. A couple of geese landed on a gravel bar. They began to honk and carry on. The crane flew, low and heavy, to the other side of the river.

"Even when it's cold, it's about the prettiest place I know of," Grayson said. "I'm sorry it took me so long to make it back to Missouri."

"You made it back exactly when you were supposed to."

Grayson nodded. "You're probably right. What about you? What is it about Clara that has you all riled up?"

"I'm not riled up. I just don't know if I can have her in my house."

Grayson grinned. "Are you worried you might be attracted to her?"

They stood there in silence.

"Well?" Grayson pushed.

He'd always been like that, pushing, prodding, poking. They'd been friends back in high school, different, but still friends. Tucker had been studious and quiet, a little bit unsure of himself. Grayson had been a charmer, full of his status as a judge's son. He'd taken some wrong turns and ended up in trouble. Tucker had kept to the straight and narrow.

Boring. He'd led a pretty boring life. He guessed having Clara around would undo that.

"I do find her attractive," Tucker admitted.

"You're so lofty," Grayson teased. "You *do* find her attractive? Who talks that way?"

"You're a real pain, you know that?" Tucker growled.

"That's more like it. Now I feel like you're a walking, talking human. A man who might find his housekeeper attractive."

"Finding her attractive isn't the problem." He stopped himself from saying more. If Clara hadn't confided in her family, he wasn't going to be the one who brought up a pregnancy she seemed to be trying to hide.

Grayson gave him a sideways look and shook his head.

"What?" Tucker asked.

Grayson managed a serious look. "Nothing."

"Really? Nothing. You talk nonstop, push your way into everyone's business, and now you have nothing to say?"

"Afraid so." Grayson lowered his voice when it became obvious the workers were listening. "Just don't hurt her."

"I'm not going to hurt her!" Tucker took a step back, surprised that he and Grayson were having this conversation. Since it was a replica of one they'd had in the not-so-distant past about Grayson and Avery.

"It doesn't feel so great, does it?" Grayson asked with a smug expression that Tucker felt an urge to wipe off his face.

"No, it doesn't. But in this case, I don't have a past, a present or a future with Clara Fisher."

"I beg to differ. You've hired her to work for you. That seems to put her in your present and your future." Grayson cocked his head to the side. "Unless you're planning on firing her right off the bat."

"I don't know what I'm planning."

"Fine, as long as you give her a chance."

"I hired her, didn't I?"

"Yeah, you did. You know, maybe you should think about dating. Meet some nice lady, settle down, have kids. Try one of those dating apps. I know other people who have used them."

Tucker rolled his eyes. "I'm not going to try a dating app."

"Well, it isn't like you're going to meet someone in Pleasant. There are more people moving out than moving in, and you're probably related to half the single women in town."

Tucker walked away, eager to end this uncomfortable conversation. He didn't discuss the women in his life, and it didn't matter if they were the women he dated or housekeepers. The subject was off-limits.

The conversation was especially off-limits with Grayson. Because he knew, no matter what, this conversation was going to circle back around to Clara Fisher.

Clara might be his housekeeper, but that didn't mean there was anything else between them.

Correction. He and Clara did have a connection. He knew her secrets. Or at least the one that was obvious. They were linked whether he liked it or not.

That didn't guarantee he wanted to keep her in his home or his life. She was complicated.

And he hated complications.

Chapter Four

"So how long will you stay in town?" Shay asked as they drove to school. They were running late because Shay had been unable to find a notebook she needed. The notebook that had been in her backpack the entire time.

"I guess it depends," Clara said. "Either I'll get my new job assignment or you'll do whatever you can to run me off. Whichever comes first."

She left out the part that mattered most, that Tucker might fire her before either of those things could happen. Good thing she didn't really need this job.

Shay had the good sense to turn red and duck her head. "I wasn't doing it on purpose."

"Weren't you?" Clara asked as she pulled up to the front of the school. "It felt as if you were. Why do you try so hard to get rid of your housekeepers?"

Shay shrugged. "I don't have to try that hard. Most of them don't want to be bothered with a teenager."

"I think you should give people a chance," Clara suggested as she shifted into Park.

"Why should I? They're hired to clean house and cook, and they're only there because he pays them."

She gave the young teenager a careful look. "Maybe they needed the work?"

Shay studied her hands that were clenched in her lap. "That's what Uncle Tucker told me. Do you need the job?"

"No, I don't. I have some savings, and I'll go back to work in the next couple of months. I'm doing this because, believe it or not, I like you."

"I thought maybe you liked Uncle Tucker," the girl said as her head popped up, and a mischievous light flickered in her hazel eyes.

"I'm going to Nan's to get cookbooks."

That brought a smile to Shay's face. It wasn't a big one, but it was a start. "Maybe tomorrow we won't have burned eggs for breakfast."

"That's my plan. But don't get your hopes up. I've never been much of a cook." And after today, she might not have a job.

Shay hitched her backpack over her shoulder and reached for the door. "I know how to cook a few things. I could help you."

"Until you run me off?" Clara teased.

A grin spread across Shay's face. "Yeah."

"Let's make a deal," Clara said wryly. "You teach me to cook, and I'll show you that I'm not going to be chased off."

Shay's hand shot out to grab Clara's in a firm handshake. "Deal."

Then she was out of the car, and Clara was left wondering why she'd agreed to take this position in the first place. Coming home wasn't as easy as she'd thought.

Being in Pleasant meant having people. The people, in this case, wanted to be involved in her life. They wanted to help, even though they didn't know what she needed help with.

As if on cue, her phone rang. She glanced at the screen as she pulled up to the stop sign. It was Nan. She probably wanted to know how she had survived the first morning. Two hours in, and Nan was already worried.

She answered. "I'm alive."

Nan chuckled. "I wondered. The girl is a sharp one, and don't ever think she isn't plotting your demise."

At that, Clara laughed. It felt good to laugh, to be distracted. "I know, she told me. How did I think I could handle a teenage girl?"

"Once upon a time you were one, so you have experience. I think she believes if she misbehaves enough, it'll drag those parents of hers back to town and back together. I wish life was that simple. If we could all just get in touch with our better selves, wouldn't the world be pretty? Unfortunately, Jana and that husband of hers are only thinking of themselves. They seem to have forgotten they have a daughter."

That statement dug into Clara's heart, because she didn't know if she could make the right decisions for the child she carried. She wanted to do what was best.

A tear rolled slowly down her cheek, warm against her skin. She swiped it away.

"Clara?" Nan reminded her that she was on the line.

"Could I borrow a cookbook?" Clara asked.

A heavy pause. "Cookbook?"

"You know I can't boil water."

"I had hoped you'd learned enough to survive. You

did take a job as a housekeeper. Did you think you'd be serving frozen pizzas to them every night?"

"I had hoped."

"Come on out. I'm home."

Home. It was the place Clara had never dreamed of having. A real home with a real parent, someone she could spend holidays with or seek out when life threw an unexpected curve ball. Her heart ached at the thought, because what had happened to her had been far more than the average curve ball. The man who had waited in the parking garage had planned his attack. He'd followed her for weeks. He'd known her schedule.

She'd thought he was a decent person, hardworking and a part of her hotel work family.

She sat at the stop sign, unable to move forward. The car behind her honked, several times. It took a minute before it actually registered that she hadn't moved. Suddenly her chest grew tight, and it hurt to breathe. She didn't see an impatient mom in a minivan, she saw him, her attacker. He'd followed her, and when she'd unlocked her car, he'd climbed in the back.

"Breathe," she told herself. "Go away, Clyde. I don't have time for you." Clyde the Elephant, her invisible nemesis anxiety. She blinked away the image that wasn't real and focused on what she knew to be true. The woman in the car zoomed around her, pulling onto the road.

Clara whispered an apology the other woman would never hear.

Her phone rang and she jumped, shaken from the memories. In slow motion she reached for the phone.

"Yes?" she answered.

"Are you okay?" Tucker, his voice deep, caring, personal.

"Of course I am." But she wasn't. How did he know?

"You don't sound fine."

He shouldn't be this involved in her life. He'd hired her as a housekeeper. End of story. "I'm good. I'm going to Nan's. Did you need something?"

"Not really." He cleared his throat. "I was driving through town and saw you sitting at the stop sign."

"Oh," she said as she looked around the area. She saw him a few hundred feet away, in his truck, sitting at another stop sign.

She couldn't see his features, just the outline of a man, but she imagined his serious expression. She could almost envision the concern in his hazel eyes. He wasn't the polished type. He was rugged, tough, kind. Her heart delved into dangerous territory. How would it feel to have a man like Tucker Church in her life?

The thought was foreign and one she couldn't allow to take root. Yes, Tucker was good and kind. But he deserved someone who came to him healthy and free of baggage. She felt splintered, as if the pieces of the person she'd once been were scattered. Putting them back together would take time.

"Meet me at Tilly's for coffee," he said.

"Coffee?"

"We should talk."

She nodded. "Of course."

She pulled out of the school parking lot and turned left, toward Tilly's. She arrived only seconds after he did, but he was already out of his truck. He met her at her car, opening the door the way he'd probably been taught a gentleman should.

"About this morning," he said at the same time that she said, "I'm sorry about this morning."

"No need to apologize," he said. "Listen, I don't know what to do. I don't know what to say."

"Right, of course. I don't expect you to say anything. I get it. This isn't what you were expecting. You need someone you can count on. You need a cook. You need a housekeeper."

"All of those things are true." He sounded apologetic.

"Let's go in for that coffee," she said. "I really could use a cup. Just one. I'm trying to break the habit."

"Of course. And it looks like it could rain."

She glanced up at the gray sky and agreed. It could rain. They entered Tilly's together, causing a few looks and whispers. Tilly came out of the kitchen, wiping her hands on a towel. She smiled when she spotted them and waved them toward an empty table.

"Have a seat, kids. I'll be right with you," said Tilly, with her gray hair pulled back with a scarf and her familiar smile. There were things in life that were constants.

They took a seat at the table for two. It was small, and their knees touched. She moved sideways, and Tucker looked awkward, a hint of red stealing into his cheeks.

"You sat at the stop sign for a long time," he said, after Tilly had poured their coffee and took their order for biscuits and gravy.

"I know." She fiddled with a sugar packet. "I called Nan to see if I could get a cookbook, and I asked her if I'd made a huge mistake, taking this job."

He grinned, flashing those dimples and a smile that could devastate a woman. Well, any woman but her.

"I thought I was the one who might have made the mistake."

She raised her gaze to meet his. "I'm sorry. It isn't that I'm trying to keep secrets. I just don't know what to tell my family."

"Is that why you're planning on leaving the country?" he asked.

"I need a new beginning."

"And Pleasant isn't that place?"

"No, it's just home."

He studied her, as if trying to figure out all of her secrets. She turned her head to look out the window.

Tilly returned with biscuits, gravy and a curious look for the two of them. "Tucker, how's that skating rink of yours coming along?"

"It's almost ready," Tucker responded. "We're opening the first weekend in December."

Tilly shook her head. "An ice rink in Pleasant. That'll put us on the map."

Tucker chuckled. "I don't know if that's true, but I hope it'll draw some visitors."

"You already did that with that river-outfitter business of yours. You know, the city council estimated that your business brought about ten thousand visitors to town last summer."

"So I heard," he said drily.

He was modest. Another thing to like about Tucker Church.

"Well, for a town of a thousand and change, that's a good number of visitors."

"It's a good start," he agreed.

"I'll leave the two of you to your breakfast." Tilly put a hand on Clara's shoulder. "I'm glad you're going to be out at the ranch. You're the right fit for Shay. She needs someone young and understanding."

Clara smiled up at Tilly but refrained from telling her that she'd probably already been fired.

"We should talk," she said, after her first bite of biscuit with Tilly's homemade sausage gravy.

"Nah, we can talk later." He pointed at his plate. "We shouldn't let this get cold."

She finished her breakfast and, true to word, they didn't discuss her situation or her job. They talked about weather, about the horses he raised and the price of cattle. The topics seemed to be the standard for Tilly's.

As she finished eating, her phone rang. "Hi, Nan. Sorry, Tucker caught up with me, and we had breakfast. No, I didn't cook. Tilly did. I'll be out shortly."

"You should go," Tucker told her after the call. "I'll catch up with you later."

"You're right, I should go. Thank you for breakfast. And for giving me a chance. I'm sorry it didn't work out."

"I thought you were going to Nan's for a cookbook?" he said as he stood and took a few bills out of his wallet.

"I was, but I didn't think…"

"We can talk later. That's all I said, Clara."

"At your place?"

He nodded and walked away, smiling as he approached the cash register where Tilly waited.

When Clara rolled up to Nan's a few minutes later, she realized they weren't going to be sitting on the back porch having coffee and discussing life. First, it was too cold. Second, she felt nauseous and suddenly coffee seemed like the worst idea ever. Third and foremost, Avery's car was parked in the drive. Avery seemed to have figured life out. She was raising an amazing daughter, who would soon be thirteen, she'd married her true love, and she had a nursing career that she loved. She'd recently taken a job at, of all places, a pregnancy center in a neighboring town.

Clara didn't want to admit it, but she was jealous of her foster sister. Not that she wanted the things Avery had, but she wanted the happiness, the contentment. The things she'd thought she possessed but were now lost. She'd find them again. She'd never been a quitter.

Nan met Clara on the back porch. "Come on in. We're just starting another pot of coffee."

At the word, Clara felt a little nauseated. She managed a smile and hoped they didn't notice. "I'm good. I've already had enough coffee today."

"I didn't know you could ever have too much coffee, but all right." Nan gave her a curious look and then she blinked. "Did you want something?"

Clara's heart nearly broke at the look of confusion and frustration on her foster mom's face.

"Just a cookbook, if you have an extra."

Nan nodded, as if she remembered. "Of course. I have a few dozen, so I'm sure we'll find one or two that you can use. You're really going to cook?"

"I don't know. But I might as well learn."

"The first day on a new job," Nan said sagely. "It'll work out."

"Yes, it'll work out." She followed Nan inside.

Avery looked up from stirring sugar in her coffee. "Everything okay?"

"Clara came by for cookbooks," Nan said.

"Yes." Avery gave Nan a reassuring look. "We'll find her something she can use."

"Kid-friendly," Nan said. "For Shay."

"Except I don't know if I still have a job," Clara said.

"Because you can't cook?" Nan asked.

Clara didn't know what to say. She looked to Avery, and Avery gave her a sympathetic look. A knowing look. She had always been observant.

She should tell them. She knew she should. Unfortunately, the words wouldn't come out. She'd tried, more than once, but each time she thought she could share what had happened, the panic would rise up. And the doubts. Would they love her if they knew she had decided she couldn't keep the baby?

"Obviously because she can't cook," Avery answered Nan. "Poor Tucker had no idea."

"I tried to warn him," Clara added. "But even if he fires me, it won't hurt me to learn to cook."

"I'm going to look and see what I have," Nan told her as she left the room.

As soon as Nan walked out of hearing range, Clara looked at Avery.

She didn't have to say a word. Avery nodded and pushed a plate of cookies in her direction. "I know. The medication she's on does help some cases. So I'm hopeful. I think it will stop the rapid progression of the dementia."

"I want it to make her better." Clara's heart ached at the thought of losing Nan. Nan was their glue. She was their everything. She'd taken a motley bunch of girls and created a family for them.

Avery studied her. "If you need anything…"

Clara closed her eyes. She felt her foster sister's hand on her arm. "I'm good."

"We have an ultrasound at the center, you know."

A shudder ran through Clara. "No. I can't talk about this. Not yet."

"It might help," Avery said. "To talk."

They could hear Nan returning. She was talking to herself about cookbooks, kids and planning meals.

"Soon," Clara assured her foster sister.

Avery gave her an understanding look, but she couldn't understand. She might think she did. She might think that Clara's situation was similar to her own, because Avery had gotten pregnant as a teenager. She'd raised Quinn on her own until Grayson had returned and realized he had a daughter.

Their situations weren't the same. She just couldn't find a way to tell her family what had happened to her. But Avery was right: it would help to talk. Soon, when she could get the words out and not break down.

As she looked over the cookbooks Nan had brought for her to choose from, she realized something. When people knew about her pregnancy, it would all become very real. Everyone would have a suggestion, a comment or an opinion about her decisions.

It was so much easier to think about pasta recipes and to laugh as Nan predicted her success with quiche. When Tucker's name was mentioned, she felt the heat of embarrassment settle in her cheeks.

"He's my boss," she reminded Nan. "The only thing I want to do is cook something that won't poison him."

Avery gave her another knowing look, a look that Clara quickly turned away from. The last thing she needed was for anyone, her family included, to think that Tucker might be more than just her employer.

* * *

Tucker got the phone call shortly after two that afternoon. His niece had decided to start a paper airplane fight in her algebra class. The teacher wasn't amused and would like Shay to go home for the day. He wasn't sure how many more of these types of days he could handle.

But because he was Tucker, and because he had spent his life doing the right thing, he said goodbye to the veterinarian he'd called for a sick cow and headed to school to pick up his niece.

As he got out of his truck, he noticed the car that pulled in next to him. Now, this was interesting. He waited for her to get out and join him on the sidewalk. She looked as surprised as he felt.

"What brings you here?" he asked, although he knew the answer.

She bit down on her bottom lip and looked a little guilty.

"Shay texted me from what she called isolation. She said she had messed up and knew she was in trouble." Clara hesitated, then looked up at him with troubled brown eyes. "I can leave if you want."

"No. She wants you here. I think that's a good thing. Unless she starts pulling more stunts just to get your attention."

Her laughter was soft, and somehow it took away the anxiety he had. The anxiety that said he shouldn't be parenting a teen.

He shouldn't have this woman in his life. The last thing he should want was her at his side as he walked into the school. But he didn't mind. He didn't mind the soft, floral scent of her perfume or even the way her fingers briefly touched his. The moment came and went so quickly he thought he might have imagined it.

Shay sat on a bench outside the principal's office. She glanced up as they approached. A smile flitted across her face, then her gaze met her uncle's, and the smile disappeared. He thought he heard her whisper, "Oops."

"You thought you'd get away with calling Clara instead of me?" he asked.

She shrugged, and if she'd looked hopeful, she now looked worried. Good, he wanted her worried. "I didn't want to bother you," she told him.

Clara gave him a slight shake of her head. He got it, or thought he did. Tread lightly. He wasn't sure if such a thing was possible. Except, for the first time in a long time he didn't feel as if he was in this alone. He had someone standing next to him.

That hadn't been the plan. He'd needed a cook and a housekeeper. Instead, he'd ended up with a woman who felt like a friend. And maybe Shay needed more than someone to fix her breakfast or wash her clothes. Maybe she needed Clara.

"Mr. Church?" the school secretary called out to him. "You can come in."

He gave his niece a warning look and stepped into the office. Clara remained behind, taking a seat on the bench next to Shay.

"I'm not sure what to do with her," he said as he entered the principal's office, closing the door so no one could hear.

Mrs. Barnes, the principal, shook her head. "I really wish there were easy answers. Shay is angry, she's hurting, but she also thinks that she's being funny when she starts this nonsense. Today she was very confused because, to her, this was all in good fun. They'd been discussing jet engines and how they work. I have a theory."

"What's that?"

"Your niece is gifted and needs more challenging work. I also want her to have something more to do with her time. I think she needs to be kept busy. Find a project. Maybe if she focused some of her energy on helping others?"

"I like that idea," Tucker agreed. Then he wondered how he would find more hours in a twenty-four-hour day. "I'll see what I can do."

"I know it's a lot," Mrs. Barnes said in a sympathetic tone. "She's a good girl. She just feels lost right now. We have a therapist that comes to the school. Would you be agreeable to Shay seeing Mindy maybe once a week?"

"I think that would be good." He would take all the help he could get.

"Tucker, it's going to work out," Mrs. Barnes reassured him. "You're doing a good job with her. And I see you've found help that probably won't turn tail and run."

When he opened the door, he could see Shay and Clara, heads bent close together as they discussed something that made Shay giggle. "Yes, I think I've found the right person."

Just that morning he'd been considering letting her go.

After a few more words with Mrs. Barnes, he joined Clara and Shay. Shay stood, hesitant. Worried about her punishment, no doubt.

"Ready to go home?" he asked.

Shay nodded and stepped next to him. Clara walked on Shay's other side. Together they left the building, braving the cool mist that fell from gray skies.

In silence they reached his truck. He opened the door for Shay, and she climbed in, avoiding looking at him.

"What about Clara?" she asked, before he closed the door.

"I have to talk to her," he answered. Shay opened her mouth to ask more questions, but he raised a hand to stop her. "I'll talk to you in a minute."

Clara had already gotten in her car. He didn't want to stand in the rain, so he opened the passenger door and joined her.

"I didn't mean to interfere," she said immediately.

"You didn't. Caring isn't interfering." He pulled off his cowboy hat and brushed a hand through his hair. "We need to find Shay something to do with her time, other than creating chaos. Something that includes helping other people."

"Is that a job offer?" she asked with a grin.

"You already had the job. I need your help with this even more than I need someone who can cook."

"I know the perfect project Shay can help with."

That sounded too good to be true. "What's that?"

"Nan takes meals to the residents of the senior-housing apartments in town. She's at home putting roast into containers and wrapping up homemade rolls. We could help her."

"That sounds perfect. Nan won't mind?"

"She won't mind," Clara assured him. "I'll meet you at her place."

He got out of her car, nodding at her through the foggy window. He hadn't fired her. She hadn't quit. He didn't know how to feel about this situation, but he was surprised that he felt pretty close to happy with the turn of events.

Now to deal with Shay.

He waited until they were on the road to speak to her. "Well, this wasn't your best day."

"I know," she admitted. "Is Clara still working for us?"

"We'll work that out later."

"If you fire her, it will be because of me." Her voice went quiet. "I mean, isn't that why everything goes wrong, because of me?"

"What?" He was driving so he couldn't give her the look he wanted to. But she sounded hurt and angry.

They were almost at Nan's. Tucker waited for a good place to pull onto the side of the road. His niece had tears streaming down her cheeks, and she turned away, trying to hide her face. She was falling apart, and he didn't know what to do. He wasn't equipped for a teen girl's tears. It was messy and heartbreaking. He opened the console of his truck and found napkins from fast-food restaurants. He shoved them at her.

"What do you mean?" he asked, keeping his voice surprisingly level. "Everything doesn't go wrong because of you. Why would you say that?"

"I heard my mom and dad arguing," she mumbled as more tears fell. "My dad said they should have waited to have kids. They could have traveled and spent more time together."

Tucker gathered Shay into his arms. "I'm really going to hurt them. Listen to me. You are the best thing they ever accomplished. They're just too blind to see how much they're missing out."

She cried into his shoulder. "I wish I didn't miss them."

"I know."

"I'm sorry I messed up your life," she sobbed into his shirt.

"You didn't mess up my life."

She nodded and pulled away from him. "I mess everything up. You can't even get work done because you have to take care of me. If I wasn't here, you wouldn't have to hire housekeepers or worry about school stuff."

"I'm not sorry you're here," he told her. And he meant it. He wasn't sorry to have her in his life. He wasn't even sorry to have hired a housekeeper who couldn't cook.

"Maybe," she said as she moved back to her seat. "But I know I'm a lot. I've heard you tell people that you're not sure what to do with me. And when are you going to date and find a wife if you're always dealing with me?"

"I don't need a wife right now. And I'm figuring this parenting thing out," he assured her. "First of all, I'm grounding you. And you're going to do a few things around town to help other people."

"Why?"

"Because it's good to help others. And maybe you won't get yourself into so much trouble."

He put his truck in gear and pulled back onto the road. "Where are we going?" Shay asked.

"To Nan's," he answered.

"Why Nan's?" Shay asked, clearly confused.

"We're starting today, serving others."

A few minutes later, Tucker pulled into Nan's driveway.

"Let's go inside." He got out of his car, glad to see that the rain had stopped. Shay joined him, and they hurried to the house.

At the back door, Clara invited them in, and they were greeted by the warmth of Nan's kitchen, the smell of roast coffee and apple pie. Nan waved them in.

"Clara told me that the two of you are going to help us deliver meals!" Nan placed a container in a box. "This will make people so happy. So many of our seniors spend a big portion of their time alone. They love company, probably more than they do my apple pie."

"What can we do to help?" Tucker asked as he moved his niece farther into the room."

"You can help me wrap the rolls." Clara motioned them to the kitchen table.

"I have a better idea," Nan cut in. "Shay can help me and Tucker can help you with those rolls. We'll get this meal on the road in no time flat."

Tucker caught the glint in Nan's eyes, the quick smile that immediately disappeared. His gaze connected with Clara's and any thoughts of objecting were forgotten, because she was Clara. Clara who dipped her head, dropping her gaze to the box of plastic wrap, as if it was the most interesting thing in the room.

"It looks like you've been hooked in to helping," she told him as she handed over the box. "Are you good with this stuff? I always make a mess of it."

"I think I'm probably an expert," he teased. "Just tell me what to do."

"Okay, Mr. Plastic Wrap expert," she smiled and lifted her chin a notch, losing the momentary shyness. "We wrap four for each apartment. If you can hand me a section of the wrap, I'll do the rest."

He took the job willingly. It meant time in this kitchen with old-fashioned gospel playing on the radio, Nan's soprano harmonizing with the musicians. It meant time spent watching Clara, trying to decipher a woman that was a puzzle. She was shy but strong, serious but funny. He enjoyed that as she worked, she would forget herself and sing along with Nan.

Only a day ago he'd offered the housekeeper job to a woman who had secrets, who couldn't cook, and who wouldn't be in the area long enough for them to even really get to know each other. Or that's what he'd thought. Yesterday.

Today he was realizing that he felt as if he already knew her, too well. The thought rattled him, and he nearly dropped the box of plastic wrap.

He realized he didn't care if she could cook. He only cared that she made his niece smile. She made him smile, too, for that matter, and that having her close meant a day that he didn't feel quite so alone.

Chapter Five

Tuesday morning, Clara woke up to her new normal. Before working for Tucker, she would wake up, take a walk, drink coffee, be sick and then go to the workshop and help Nan with her boats. Now the schedule omitted the walk, included gulping coffee and hoping she could keep said coffee down while hurrying to Tucker's.

As she drove down the river road, she took in the beauty of the place she called home. Pleasant was a town that time had forgotten. It boasted a grocery store, sandwich shop, convenience stores, Tilly's Café, the obligatory small-town flea market, as well as a boutique clothing store and a gift shop.

A short distance from town she turned onto the country road that led to Tucker's farm. She parked near the house, greeted Dudley as he lumbered across the yard to join her, then hurried up the steps to knock on the door.

The door opened, and Shay stood there, a big smile on her face. Clara returned that gesture, but she wasn't fooled. Shay wanted her there but also wanted her gone. Years ago, Clara had felt the same way about Nan. She'd wanted the love and acceptance of her foster mom.

She'd also spent time pushing her away, testing her, waiting for her to mess up or give up.

"I have to go to school today," Shay informed her with a frown as she motioned Clara inside.

"That's typically what happens on a Tuesday in November. What would you like for breakfast?" Clara asked. She'd come armed with cookbooks, but none of them had any easy breakfast recipes.

As they walked to the kitchen, Shay chatted about school and things she wanted to learn to do. Clara listened, trying to keep up with the rapid dialogue of the teenager.

"Morning," the now familiar, gruff but kind voice greeted her as she entered the kitchen.

Clara raised her gaze to meet Tucker's. He was pouring water into the coffee maker, but he hesitated for a moment, watching her as she entered his kitchen.

He towered over her, making her feel small, yet not afraid. At least not the kind of afraid that could send her into a fearful panic. Tucker, with his outdoorsy scent, a mixture of fresh air, hay and pine, was a whole different kind of frightening.

He gave her a questioning look but he remained silent. The look slid between them but the moment evaporated when Shay cleared her throat.

"I need breakfast," she announced with a smirk.

Right. Breakfast for Shay. That was, after all, Clara's reason for being here.

The girl who leaned against the counter was in need of someone who would care for her, guide her, feed her. Clara needed to get her act together and do the job she'd been hired to do.

That didn't include mooning over Tucker Church.

"Eggs," she said into the silence, taking them all by surprise. "I'll make scrambled eggs and toast. If that suits you all?"

"Are you sure?" Tucker asked, looking very skeptical.

"You doubt me?"

"Only a little."

He pulled a pan out of the cabinet and set it on the six burner gas stove. He leaned against the counter and motioned to the kitchen.

"It's all yours."

Shay had disappeared. Now what? Eggs were easy, weren't they? She opened cabinets until she found a small mixing bowl and cracked an egg, dropping the contents into the bowl.

"Are you going to stay and supervise?" she asked, giving him a side-eye as she cracked a second egg. A piece of shell dropped into the bowl.

He handed her a spoon, and she chased the brown shell around until she fished it out.

"I'm not supervising," he told her with a grin that unsettled her. "I'm observing."

"Being entertained is more like it," she shot back.

He chuckled. "Maybe a little. Would you like milk?"

"For what?"

"I can't believe Nan let you leave home without learning to cook," he teased as he opened the fridge door and pulled out the milk.

"Oh, she tried. I can build you a Jon boat from the bottom up, guide you on a trip down the river, catch you a decent mess of fish and even start a fire. She couldn't teach me to cook. But don't worry, I'm older now. I'm sure it'll be fine."

"Now I'm worried. But at least I know, if all else fails, you can catch some fish. You didn't mention cooking the fish."

"Nan always fried the fish."

He poured milk into the eggs and handed her a fork. She took the hint and stirred the eggs and milk together. There was salt on the counter. She grabbed it and gave a little shake into the egg mixture. He'd returned with shredded cheese, and he dropped a handful into the eggs.

"Might as well go all the way," he said.

She smiled as she glanced into the bowl, then wished she hadn't looked. A wave of nausea rolled through her stomach, catching her by surprise. Hand to her mouth, she ran from the room.

When she returned, Tucker was at the stove, spatula in one hand, a cup of coffee in the other. She hesitated in the doorway and watched for a moment. He was so cute with his short but curly hair, black-frame glasses perched on his straight and perfect nose. He was dressed for a day of farm work, in a gray button-up shirt, jeans and boots. He looked like a mix of banker and cowboy.

"Feel better?" he asked, without looking at her.

"No," she replied. "I feel terrible because once again I've proven I'm not the best person for this job."

He flipped the scrambled eggs, stirred them a bit and turned the burner down. Finally he glanced her way, and she was devastated by the look of concern in his hazel eyes. He set his cup down and pulled off his glasses, shoving them in the pocket of his shirt.

"You are the best person for this job," he said simply. "We'll work out the cooking arrangement somehow, but Shay needs you."

"Thank you," she said, her voice growing tight with emotion.

"Don't cry," he warned. "I'm a sympathy crier. One tear and I'm going to have to hug you."

"I …" She bit back the words.

Tucker turned back to the eggs, pretending they needed his attention. "This is ready. Are you hungry?"

"Not really. I'll get plates and put the toast in for the two of you."

"Already done," he said.

"This is why I'm an amazing supervisor," she quipped.

He chuckled, the sound sliding over her, warming her heart.

"What's for breakfast?" Shay skipped into the room at that moment, dissolving whatever had been building between them.

"Scrambled eggs," Tucker and Clara responded simultaneously.

Shay gave them a curious look as she packed her lunch. Tucker poured himself another cup of coffee.

"I think you really don't need a cook," Clara said. "You're pretty self-sufficient."

"He's afraid of teen girls. You're the buffer." Shay zipped her lunch box and winked at Clara. "Will you be driving me to school?"

"I don't know, you kind of scare me, too." Clara teased as she handed Shay a plate. "Eat something."

"You're only a little afraid," Shay said. "I've been thinking. Could we bake cookies? For the people at senior housing, I mean. They were all so happy to get food. I bet they'd love to have chocolate chip cookies."

"What a great idea," Clara quickly said before Tucker

could tell his niece it was a bad idea. Shay wasn't the only one who needed something to take her mind off her troubles.

Tucker gave her a careful look. "Are you sure?"

She followed the unspoken implication in the question. Was she up to this? The last thing she wanted was for him to feel sorry for her or to think she couldn't do the job he'd hired her to do. Well, obviously she couldn't do the job. He'd just cooked breakfast instead of her doing it.

"Of course I'm sure. I'll—" Suddenly her phone rang. She glanced at the caller ID. It was Avery.

"Answer it," he told her. "Shay, please finish breakfast. You can't be late to school. And you also need to make better choices today."

Shay sighed. "I'll make good choices. I never mean to make bad ones. It's just…"

The conversation faded as Clara listened to her foster sister explain the situation. The ladies were at church going through costumes for an upcoming program, and they needed a seamstress. Clara had always loved to sew, so of course they thought she might be able to help.

Avery didn't give her time to voice any objections. "It won't take long. It's less than a dozen costumes that need to be cut down to fit children."

"I'll help," Clara said.

"Would you be able to come by this morning?"

"Yes, after I drop Shay off at school, I'll head your way." She ended the call and turned to Tucker. "Do you mind?"

"Not at all. I left a list on the fridge. Groceries, laundry, the bathrooms. But I do want Shay to help with the chores."

Clara plucked the list from the fridge and gave it a look. "We can handle this. I'll add cookie ingredients and pick them up with the other items you need from the store."

"Thank you," the big cowboy said, humble and kind.

She had to stop thinking of him that way, or any way. Period. The last thing she needed was to form some silly sentimental attachment to this place and this man. He was kind for giving her a job, something to keep her mind off her troubles. End of story.

She glanced at the clock on the coffee maker. "We should go."

"Yes, we should." Tucker tossed Shay her backpack. "Don't forget that. I'll be at the campground this morning and back here this afternoon."

"Oh, Shay, do I pick you up from school, or do you ride the bus home?"

"Bus in the afternoon. I like to ride because I sit with my friends," Shay explained as she gave Tucker a quick hug. "Let's go."

Yes, let's, Clara thought. She hurried out the back door, eager to leave behind her boss, the confusion and the temptation.

By midafternoon, Tucker had replaced a section of fencing that he'd been meaning to repair for the past year. He and his hired hand, Eddie, had made quick work of the project. After finishing up, he gave Eddie a list of things he'd like to get done before the end of the week. He left the teenager with the farm truck and tools that needed to be put back in the barn, and he headed for the house.

After washing up, he put on a pot of coffee and

headed to his office just off the kitchen. It was a pretty decent day for late November, and the last thing he wanted was to be stuck in the house, but the campground wouldn't run itself.

What had started as a fun hobby, a lifelong dream, had become a serious business. Who knew that putting some canoes in the river for tourists and adding a few camping spots on the riverbank would turn in to something that drew people from all over the country?

The James River was no white water rafting experience, it was just a slow and easy float trip with gravel bars for picnics and some pretty bluffs and tree-covered hills that were home to deer, eagles and other wildlife. The river had once been a place where mainly locals camped and fished. Now it was a place for city folks to get away and experience nature.

The problem that faced him today was planning a glamping site. The back door opened, taking him by surprise. He looked up, the surprise growing when he realized it was Clara, her arms loaded with bags of groceries. He'd somehow forgotten that she'd be returning this afternoon.

He growled at the paper in front of him, trying to focus on making notes about things that needed to be done before Christmas and before spring. It was her fault. She had that look about her, a sprite, a pixie, a fresh-faced girl from the country. She turned him inside out with those soulful brown eyes and the honey-blond curls that hung to her shoulders and framed her face. She was a living, breathing country song about heartbreak, that's what she was. And he knew all about heartbreak. Well, not big heartbreak. The normal teen stuff.

He wasn't a man who normally had poetic thoughts, like comparing a woman to a country song.

"Why are you frowning? Wasn't I supposed to come back?" she asked as she left bags of groceries on the table and headed his way.

"I'm not frowning," he said as he turned his attention back to his work. He adjusted his glasses and glared at the paper. He hadn't known she was around. Good thing he hadn't been talking to himself.

"You are frowning. I'm going to get a complex," she teased.

He raised his gaze to hers and smiled.

"Not helping," she said. She sat down next to him and studied the papers. "What's all this?"

"Glamping."

"Oh, glamping." She laughed softly, the noise making him want to pull her close. "What's *glamping*?"

"Glamorous camping?" he said, making it a question when it wasn't. At least it gave him something to think about other than how pretty she looked in the deep red sweater she wore.

"You don't know for sure?" She had her phone out and was searching the term.

"I do know. But what does a hillbilly farmer from the Ozarks know about *glamour*? Especially when the word is used in connection to tents and camping. My idea of camping is a sleeping bag on the gravel bar, a big fire and fried fish."

"Mine, too," she admitted.

"Really?"

"What? You think I can't do hard-core camping? I grew up in a house that had holes in the walls and sometimes no electricity for months on end."

He didn't know how to respond.

"Stop overthinking. I wasn't telling you that to make you feel bad. I can rough it, though."

"I have no doubt," he replied, seeing her in a new light.

"But about this glamping stuff," she redirected them back to their main topic of conversation. "I do know what it is. I'm just trying to picture how it translates to the James River and Pleasant, Missouri."

"That is the million-dollar question."

As she leaned over to glance at his notes, he noticed again that she smelled flowery. He tried not to inhale her scent: that would be too obvious and probably downright rude. He was a gentleman, born and raised. His mama had taught him to open doors, buy flowers and treat a woman with respect.

Lately he'd been feeling like a lot of women didn't like gentlemen. They liked the rowdy men of his acquaintance, heartbreakers. For what it was worth, he thought they were barking up the wrong trees.

"Interesting," she said. "Look at these amazing tents at that resort down south of Branson. Those are spectacular. Is that what you're planning?"

She held her phone out to show him pictures he'd seen before. White tents on the edge of the lake, decks overlooking the water, privacy fences, outdoor bathtubs, firepits.

"I don't have the kind of money for that type of setup, and also the river and the lake are worlds apart when it comes to planning and lodging. I'd love to have these close to the river, but flooding is an issue. I'd love to have the decks overlooking the water, but then I worry about children."

"So what you're saying is that your glamping sites needs to be mobile and your decks need to be safe?"

"I hadn't thought of that. I was thinking tents that could quickly be taken down, but not really mobile."

"It would be more expensive to put them on concrete, and concrete can take a hit if the river floods. Why not put them on a frame that can sit on a foundation of blocks or have wheels attached should there be the threat of a flood. You can still do the cozy fires, the chairs, the decks that can actually be a part of your frame. The difference is, at the threat of flood, you load it all up and pull it to higher ground."

He wanted to kiss her. She was not only pretty, she was smart.

"I like it. We could try one, made with cheaper materials, just to see how it would work." He studied her notes. "I couldn't charge the big prices, like this lake resort, but I think it could be profitable."

"So do I. If you want, I could study this and the best ways to market them."

"I would appreciate that," he answered as he got up from his chair and moved away from her.

Her hand went to her belly, staying there for only a few seconds and then drifting away as she drew in a breath.

"Are you okay?" he asked, maintaining the distance between them. "You know, if you need to talk…"

She stared at the paper in front of her. "I don't, but thank you. I should get the rest of the things out of the car and start dinner."

"I can help," he started.

She shook her head. "It's just a few things."

She avoided eye contact as she escaped.

He let her go, knowing it was the right decision in this situation. She worked for him in a temporary position. That was as far as their relationship needed to go.

Less than a minute later, he changed his mind and followed her out the back door to her car. Her back was to him, and she was grabbing reusable bags full of groceries.

"Let me help you carry these in," he told her.

She shook her head, keeping her back to him. "Please, just go inside."

She was crying. He could hear it in her voice. Tucker touched her arm. She flinched, jerking away from him.

"Don't touch me," she warned.

"I won't hurt you," he said as he withdrew his hand. "Clara, I promise I'm not going to hurt you."

She trembled as he stepped closer. Her eyes fluttered closed. She put a hand up to stop him from moving closer.

"I know you won't, but I need a moment."

Then a startling thing happened. Clara, still holding a cloth bag in each hand, stepped into his arms, burrowing against his shoulder, her tears drenching his shirt. He hesitated, unsure how to proceed. As she continued to cry, he pulled her close and held her.

He couldn't not hold her.

The thing he knew, almost with certainty, was that he was the first person to hold her in a very long time. And letting go of her might possibly be the most difficult thing he would ever have to do.

Chapter Six

Saturday mornings at Tilly's were busy. People gathered at the local diner for breakfast, gossip and, in the case of the ladies from Pleasant Community Church, weekly Bible study. Clara sat at the long table near the back of the dining room with Nan, Avery, Tilly and several others who were discussing life, the Bible and the price of gas over coffee cups and empty plates.

Tilly hopped up and went to the register. After all, she could study the Bible, but that didn't mean old Daniel Allen was going to wait around to pay his tab. He'd already hollered from across the diner that he had cattle to work and couldn't wait all day for Tilly to stop yammering with her ladies' group.

Someone's phone rang. It had one of those annoying ringtones. The ladies looked at each other, waiting for someone to realize it belonged to them. Avery pulled the offending phone out of a purse on the floor. She held it up.

"Mary?"

Mary Alton was Tilly's twin. Her cheeks turned pink as she reached for the phone. "Goodness me. I don't know why I have that ringtone. I'm going to blame that on Bo."

Her husband was a practical joker.

"Mary, answer your phone." Avery swiped the screen of the phone and pushed it to Mary's ear, ending the chorus of a song that had belonged to a seventies one-hit wonder.

"Oh, right. Yes. Hello?" Mary answered, and for a moment the conversation at the table went silent. They had no choice. Mary was loud, but even louder when talking on the phone. "No, I didn't see that they were having a sale. Well, I might need some chicken feed and maybe sunflower seeds for my birds."

Around the table, there was a quiet chorus of giggles.

She finally ended the call. "That was Bo, letting me know Farm and Home is having a sale."

"Do they have bird feeders on sale, too?" Betty Darby asked.

"I'm not sure. We might have to drive by on our way home," Mary answered.

Conversations started again. And Clara wished she'd stayed at Nan's. Where it would be silent and peaceful. Where she could sit on the patio and watch the river wind its way through the hills. At home Clyde the Elephant could have been banished with ease. The moment she felt his weight, she would have gotten up to do something or gone for a walk.

The topic bounced around from bananas at the grocery to how Bo had pranked Mary the night before. Mary smiled as if she would never tire of the man's silly jokes.

Clara glanced at her watch. Finally she had a reason to leave. "I have to go."

Nan gave her a curious look. "Where are you off to?"

She started to remind Nan that she'd already told her, but instead, she repeated herself. "I'm going to watch Shay. We're baking cookies today."

Nan's eyes scrunched, then she nodded. "I remember you mentioning that. I also have something to do today." She looked at Avery.

"We're going to the church to help decorate for Christmas," Avery supplied.

Nan glanced away, but not before Clara saw the sheen of tears. Avery caught Clara's attention, and the two of them shared a solemn moment. For more than a decade, Nan had mothered them. She'd paid for dance lessons, cheered at sporting events and graduation, encouraged them in their less-than-stellar moments, telling them everything would work out.

Nan had helped them believe in themselves and in a faith much larger than themselves. Now it was their turn to play that role for her.

"Will you be home later?" Nan asked.

Clara grabbed her purse, her bill for breakfast, as well as Nan's, and hugged her foster mom. "Yes, I'll be home."

She made quick eye contact with Avery and saw the concern in her foster sister's expression. She wasn't surprised when Avery followed her. She waited as Clara paid, and then they walked together out the front door.

"You're very obvious," Clara said as she hit the button to unlock her car.

Avery chuckled. "Do you think anyone noticed?"

"Everyone noticed." Clara opened the car door and waited for Avery to say what was on her mind.

"I just wanted to make sure you're okay. And I want you to know I'm here if you need me."

Wasn't that why she'd come home? To be with her family, this assorted bunch of women, none related by blood but all a part of her heart. Hadn't she come home to find rest in the presence of God, because He had been her help, her shelter for a lifetime of painful events?

"I know you're here," she assured her sister. "That's why I came home. Don't worry, I'm not falling apart. Not yet. I'm trying to put the pieces back together."

Avery hugged her. "If you need anything at all..."

"You're here for me. You always have been. And now, I have to get to Tucker's. I promised Shay we would make cookies or candy, maybe both."

They parted, and Clara backed out of the parking lot and headed toward Tucker's place. Clyde the Elephant didn't make an appearance. He knew better. She had peace like a river, as the old song said. Today she was spending time with a teenager who needed a friend. Decisions for her own future were pushed firmly to the back of her mind.

Five minutes after leaving the diner, she pulled up to Tucker's. In the distance she saw him as he left the barn and headed for the equipment shed. He waved and she waved back, because she couldn't pretend she hadn't seen him.

Shay greeted her as she entered through the back door. She tossed Clara an apron.

"Nice to see you, too."

"Cookie baking time," Shay said with a big grin.

"And yet you're dressed like someone who has been

in the woods cutting firewood," Clara pointed out. Shay wore a flannel shirt, jeans and work boots.

"We were at the river, watching the guys string the Christmas lights for the ice rink. Uncle Tucker is going to have a drive-through light display. He's going to take donations and give the money to the church to help people at Christmas. It was my idea."

"I think that's a great suggestion." Keeping Shay busy was key to keeping her mind off her parents. She ignored the fact that she, too, needed to keep her mind off her troubles.

She was having a baby.

The baby of a man who had violently attacked her and left her broken and sobbing. A baby that she didn't plan to raise. She blinked away the memory and managed a smile for Tucker's niece.

"Are you sick?" Shay asked, observant and thoughtful.

"I'm fine." She smiled to prove it. "Let's get those cookies started."

"Where do we start?" Shay asked, still watching her closely, as if seeking signs of illness.

"I've been told that a recipe is a good place."

"I second that," Tucker's deep voice answered.

Clara smiled at him. Standing just inside the back door, his ball cap was tipped at an angle that lent boyish charm to his face. Clara glanced away as he pulled off his flannel jacket and dropped it on a hook by the door, along with the ball cap.

"We just happen to have recipes," Clara reassured him. "Are you here to help us?"

"I thought I might." He winked at them. "Believe it

or not, I'm a pretty decent hand when it comes to making cookies."

"I don't doubt that," Clara answered. "But I'd hate to take you away from something you need to be doing."

He gave her a long look. "Are you trying to get rid of me?"

"Not at all." Although, there was something so unsettling about his presence. Something that made her wish her life could be different. He made her want things that she'd never considered for herself. A home, a family, a future with someone strong and steady.

"Butter. We probably need butter." Shay broke the awkward silence, giving the two of them a look before she opened the refrigerator. "What else?"

"Sugar, both kinds. Vanilla, flour, eggs, baking soda." Clara perused the recipe in the cookbook she'd opened.

"Chocolate chips." Tucker pulled the bag out of the cabinet. "You at least need me for the things you can't reach."

"We have a step stool," Clara teased.

"I almost never burn things," he shot back.

"That's low." Clara feigned hurt. "I can't believe you'd go for my weak spot."

"In love and war…" He stumbled over the words and turned red in the face.

"All is fair."

Shay pretended to gag, but then she pulled a mixing bowl out of the cabinet and recovered by eating a few of the chocolate chips.

"Sugars and butter first," Shay said, referring to the recipe. She measured and poured the ingredients into a bowl. "I always wanted to make cookies. We always just bought the premade dough."

"That's good, too," Clara offered. "When they come out of the oven, warm and chewy, it doesn't much matter if they're homemade or not."

"Sure, it matters," Shay said.

"Eggs," Clara read the next ingredient and glanced at Tucker. "I think you should do that. We don't want egg shells in the cookies."

"You trust me to add the eggs?" he said.

"I trust you," she said. She had to look away because this felt too much like flirting.

"I hope the people at the senior housing like our cookies," Shay said as they mixed in the dry ingredients.

"I'm sure they will," Clara assured her as she pulled out the baking sheets. "Drop the dough on the sheets by spoonfuls, Shay. That's your job."

"Did you know that Joe and Donna in apartment twelve have no children?" Shay asked as she plopped a blob of dough onto the pan. "They used to, but their daughter died twenty-five years ago. They moved here and didn't know anyone, but they love Pleasant and their neighbors. And Marty Molder, she's alone. Her kids moved away, and she doesn't have any family left in town. She helps Mr. Jackson because he has a hard time taking care of himself."

"You learned all of this while we gave out meals with Nan?" Clara asked.

Shay nodded as she filled up the cookie sheet and Clara slid it into the oven.

"They like to have someone to talk to," Shay told

them. "When we were there the other day, I just listened while they talked."

Clara smiled at the girl. "Shay, that's a beautiful skill to have, listening to others. Don't ever lose that."

Shay shrugged as if it was nothing, and maybe at her age it didn't seem important. It was a gift, though. People wanted to be listened to. Listening was a sign of caring.

She had people in her life who wanted to listen, and she hadn't let them in. She knew she would have to rectify that, but what would they think of her when they found out what she'd decided about the future of the baby growing inside her?

Would they understand why she'd decided to give her baby up for adoption? She wanted her child to have a loving family, people who were nurturing and would provide a stable homelife. Would her family and friends understand that she didn't know if she could hold this child when it would mean looking into the eyes of the man who had attacked her?

Shay continued to tell stories of people they'd met at the senior-housing complex. Clara walked around the counter to sit on a barstool as a sharp pain slid through her abdomen. She pulled the now-cool cookie sheet to her and transferred the cookies to a cooling rack. Tucker gave her a questioning look, because of course he noticed. Shay pretended to not notice that Clara had taken a seat.

The pain eased, and she breathed a sigh of relief. No matter what, the child growing inside her was an innocent life. She wanted the baby to be okay, to be healthy. She looked up and caught Tucker studying her.

Clara had been on her own for most of her life. She'd

hidden so much, from teachers, from friends, even from Nan. Hiding her pain had become second nature.

The desire to share with this man, a man she barely knew, took her by surprise. Why Tucker? Why now?

Tucker watched Clara from the corner of his eye as he dug in a drawer and found a notebook for Shay, who had just pulled a still-warm chocolate chip cookie off the rack. It fell apart as she put it in her mouth.

"Write down your ideas for helping people. As you think of things make a list, and we'll see what we can do to make Christmas a happier time for some of these people."

"We could have a Christmas dinner here, with little gifts and pies. Nan makes the best pies." Shay grabbed a pen to jot down her ideas.

"That's a start. Remember, keep it doable."

"Doable?" Shay asked.

"We have a pretty full plate during the holidays, and I want to make sure we have ideas we can follow through on."

"Got it," Shay said. "Doable."

"Once you have a list, we'll put together a plan." Tucker gave Clara another look. He'd noticed a moment ago she seemed to be in pain. "When are we delivering these cookies?"

"Tomorrow," Shay answered. "We're going to deliver them tomorrow after church. Tilly gave us to-go containers to put them in."

"While the two of you finish the cookies, I'm going to bring Christmas decorations up from the basement."

Shay's eyes lit up. "You got the tree? The one I showed you?"

"Yes, I got that tree. I hope you like it. It's a cedar tree so it isn't perfectly shaped, but it does smell good."

"I'll love it. And lights. Don't forget lights."

He shook his head at her. "You've gotten very bossy."

Shay smiled. "I'm also a good sandwich maker. I think we should have sandwiches for lunch."

"Grilled cheese," Clara said.

"And tomato soup," Shay added.

Tucker could hear them as he went down the stairs to the basement. They were laughing and shrieking about burnt cookies. The sounds of laughter and happiness followed him. For the first time in a long time he believed Shay would be okay. Unfortunately, Clara wouldn't stay. What would they do when she left?

He took advantage of the time alone in the basement to pray, because hiring Clara had complicated his life, and that was the last thing he needed.

When he returned with a tub of decorations, Shay and Clara were putting sandwiches on a griddle, and the soup was steaming in the pan. Clara stirred the soup, then spotted him.

"Lunch is ready," she said.

"It smells good," he told her.

Clara grinned. "I'm not a gourmet cook, but I can open a can of soup. With Shay's help."

She should smile more often. He wanted to know her better, so he could ask what had caused the dark shadows in her eyes, the loss of her smile.

"I'll have to go soon," Clara told Shay as they finished lunch.

"Go? But we're going to decorate the tree. Maybe we could make hot chocolate?" Shay looked to him, as if imploring him to make Clara stay.

"Shay," Tucker warned. It was a half-hearted attempt, because he found that he wasn't in a big hurry to see Clara leave. He liked his house, and his life, with her in it.

"Fine," Shay said in a tone that said it was less than okay with her, but she knew better than to keep it up.

"I'm going to get the tree and put it in a stand. Do we want it in a living-room window?" he asked as he headed for the back door to get the tree he'd left in his truck.

"That's perfect," Shay told him as she loaded the dishwasher. She was helping out and hadn't been asked. Would wonders never cease?

Clara stood at the refrigerator. He hadn't noticed before but now he did. She'd hesitated, one hand on the handle and the other on her belly. She grimaced and closed her eyes, just briefly. When she opened her eyes, she noticed him watching and quickly glanced away. He went out the door, because he knew she didn't want him involved in that part of her life.

Tucker unloaded the prickly evergreen and then leaned it against the back of his truck. The scent of cedar sprung up around him. A store-bought tree, maybe a pretty fir or spruce, would have been nicer, probably less likely to fall apart. But Shay had wanted the cedar, and he didn't blame her. Cedar trees always looked and smelled like Christmas to him. Maybe because that's what he'd grown up with. Every year they'd gone out and picked a tree from the field for his dad to cut down. He missed his parents. He knew they were working hard in the mission field, but he'd give anything if they could come home for Christmas.

He pulled on gloves and reached through the

branches to get a good hold on the trunk in order to carry it to the house.

Tucker took the tree to the living room where he worked on setting it up in the tree stand. From there he could make out snippets of conversation. They were wrapping cookies and placing them in the containers. He heard them discussing placing the containers in the pantry. A few minutes later he heard Clara explaining to Shay that she had to leave. Nan would be at home and they had a few things to do at her place.

When he returned to the kitchen, they were washing mixing bowls and measuring cups they'd used for the cookies. The kitchen was spotless, and there was no sign of cookies.

"Hey, where did they all go?" he asked.

Shay pushed a plate across the counter. "We saved some for you."

"Very kind of you." He bit into a cookie, and he couldn't help but watch Clara. With a damp hand she pushed her hair back from her face, leaving behind a few bubbles of dish soap.

"I'm going now," she informed him as she grabbed her purse. "See you tomorrow at church."

"I'll walk you out," Tucker replied, the unplanned offer taking him by surprise. She had a way of bringing out a spontaneous side he hadn't known he possessed.

"You don't have to," she told him. That didn't surprise him.

"I want to," he said. He gave his niece a look. "Go ahead and pick the decorations you want to use."

Shay had been standing at the counter, eating another cookie. He wondered how many she'd had. She ran to Clara, nearly knocking her off balance as she wrapped her in a hug.

"Thank you for making cookies with me," his niece said.

"Of course," Clara said. "I enjoyed it."

She gave Shay a quick hug and said goodbye. Tucker had to hurry to catch up with her as she headed out the door. He was determined to walk her to her car.

"You don't have to accompany me."

"My mom raised me to be a gentleman. You seemed a little under the weather, and I was worried about you."

She huffed a little at that. Then she stopped and faced him. "I'm not your responsibility. No matter what you think of my situation, I'm handling it. I'm good."

He raised his hands in pseudo-surrender. "I'm only trying to be a friend."

Her face crumpled. No tears but she looked about to cry. He wasn't the best with women in distress. When Shay had first come to him, he'd found that he could do an awkward pat on the back. He'd moved on to the side hug. He'd learned to be a bit more comforting than that, but it was still a work in progress.

"You're kind, Tucker. You're a wonderful, decent man. You're more decent than any man I think I've ever known."

That left him speechless. The compliment was sweet and maybe a way to keep him at a distance. He was kind. Isn't that what women said to men they wanted to keep as a friend but nothing more? He took her hand and walked with her the remaining distance to her car. She looked at their joined hands but didn't pull away from him.

"Thank you," she whispered. "For being so kind."

"Being kind is no longer in vogue," he said ruefully, and yet, wasn't it the truth?

"What does that mean?" she asked.

He looked at their joined hands. Slowly he raised her hand to his lips and placed a light kiss on her palm.

"Women, it seems, like the bad boys." He winked, to keep the conversation light. "I've tried that route, and it fit like new boots that hadn't been broken in. Not my style."

"Don't change," she told him. "I like Tucker Church because he is good and decent. Someday the right woman will come along. It'll happen when you're least expecting it." She laughed a little.

"You think that's funny?" he asked, a bit hurt.

"No, not at all. I just realized, I'm the last person who should be giving you advice." She kissed his hand back and then rested her cheek on their joined hands, just for a moment. "Thank you for being my friend."

"I think this is what the younger crowd calls being friend-zoned?" he asked.

"It's really all you want from me, Tucker." Her hand went to her belly. "I think for obvious reasons."

"Just remember, I'm here if you need anything. I think we've established that I make a decent friend."

"You do." She reached for her car door, but he beat her to it and opened it for her. She smiled up at him as she got in and he closed it for her.

As she drove away, he lectured himself for having said all the wrong things. Not that it mattered. He had a full plate, and she wasn't interested. If he had any sense at all, he'd keep his distance from Clara Fisher.

Instead he'd placed her front and center in his life. He would see her every day, worry about her, care about her. All of the things he hadn't wanted to do because he'd known from the beginning that she could easily win a piece of his heart.

Chapter Seven

Clara made it through the entire Sunday morning church service. She sat with her family, the family that God had given her, and she felt more peace than she had in months. A few pews ahead of them, Tucker sat with Shay, his uncle Dallas, and several other people whom she'd met over the years but didn't really know.

She made a conscious effort not to stare at the back of Tucker's head, at the light brown curls that were streaked with blond from the summer sunshine. She tried not to notice the massive breadth of his shoulders. Most importantly she didn't dwell on the way it had felt the previous day when he had drawn her hand to his lips for a gentle kiss. In the first moments of that gesture, she'd felt Clyde take a seat on her chest, his heavy weight a reminder of the anxiety that had become too familiar since the attack. As she'd met Tucker's tender gaze, something amazing had happened: she'd felt more than the anxiety, she'd felt a stirring of something sweet and precious. She'd trusted him, trusted his touch.

The service ended. He glanced behind him, and their eyes met. Heat crawled up her cheek, and she looked away, giving her attention to Avery. The knowing glint in her foster sister's eyes brought a second wave of embarrassed heat.

"Caught," Avery whispered.

"You caught nothing."

Avery giggled, the way she did when they were teens, sharing secrets under the stairs of Nan's house.

"Will you stay and help with the music for the Christmas program?" Avery asked. "I'm not a musician, and I always struggle putting together this part of the program."

"I'm not a musician, either," Clara objected.

"Yes, you are," Avery told her. "I'll buy you lunch tomorrow."

"One of Tilly's salads and a piece of chess pie?" Clara bargained, finding it easy to smile.

"Yes, whatever you want."

"Okay, I'll help. Let me tell Nan."

Nan joined them. "I'm staying to help with costumes. We'll have a quick lunch, and then we'll get busy."

Clara looked heavenward before facing her foster sister again. "I never had a choice, did I?"

"Sure, you did," Avery assured her. "If you hadn't wanted to help, I would have driven you home."

"To a solitary lunch of guilt over easy?" Clara teased, finding she really wasn't truly offended by the maneuvering. This was all normal. It was family.

She'd needed these people, this town and her church where she felt God and knew that He would heal her heart.

They moved away from the small group that surrounded them. Avery guided her in the direction of the door.

"We're practicing in the youth building," Avery explained as they walked outside. The day was crisp, cool, gray. Typical early December in southwest Missouri. "There's lunch, too. One of the men ordered subs from the store."

"I'm not really hungry," Clara said as they walked in the direction of the multipurpose building a short distance from the church.

"How are you feeling?" Avery asked.

Clara nodded. "As good as can be expected."

"Do you need anything?"

Clara thought about that for a few moments. "A trip back in time would be good."

"What happened?" Avery asked, her voice soft.

They'd reached the activity building, and rather than go in, they walked the other direction, away from the door. The winter grass crunched beneath their feet, and a flock of mourning doves cooed and scattered as they approached. Clara swallowed the lump of emotion that lodged in her throat. The cool December air brushed across her face, and the tears that were streaking down her cheeks turned cold. She brushed them away and sniffled.

"You don't have to talk. If someone broke your heart, I've been—"

"No," Clara said, cutting her off. "My heart hasn't been broken."

Her life had been broken.

"Clara?" Avery prodded.

She wanted to open up, but she'd never been good at sharing her life, her secrets. She wanted to share the nightmare with someone other than a police officer, a doctor or a hospital social worker. But she couldn't. Not yet.

"I'm okay," she lied. But it wasn't really a lie. It had been months ago, and each day that went by brought her a little closer to healing. The nightmares were fewer and further apart. Clyde still showed up on occasion, but she could get in her car now and not fear shadows or the dark.

"Okay, but you know I'm here if you need me."

"I know you're here, and I do appreciate you. I just can't do this all at once." Clara gave her a quick hug. "I love you. Never doubt that. Never doubt that you're my favorite sister."

"I love you back," Avery said as she flicked away a tear that streaked down her cheek.

They entered the building, and Clara excused herself. "I need to wash my face."

She needed some quiet, just for a moment, to compose herself.

When she returned to the main room, a group of children were onstage practicing a musical nativity. A group of shepherds were just stepping forward to sing. Clara joined Avery at the front of the stage, pretending she didn't notice Tucker working on the set, attaching a star to the wall behind the children.

Clara listened to the children but she couldn't help but look at the star, or possibly the man hanging it. She knew better. She knew there wasn't room for a relationship. Right now was about her, about healing and finding her path.

The shepherd song ended, and the play continued with angels, wise men riding camel props, and a baby in a manger. Both actors playing Joseph and Mary were children, and they took their roles so seriously that it sent a shiver down Clara's spine.

Or perhaps it was a reaction to the thought of Mary and her child, the baby Jesus. A child Mary hadn't expected. A child Joseph didn't know how to accept.

Clara touched her belly, now starting to grow round with child. A child she hadn't expected. One she didn't know how to accept. One she planned to send away, so that they could have a home with two parents who could love them unconditionally.

Shay moved to the side of the stage as Mary and Joseph stood, the baby-doll Jesus held close. Shay held a microphone in her hands and began to sing a song about Mary and her child.

The teenager hit a wrong note, and her face showed that she'd heard it. She sought Clara, their gazes locking. Clara nodded, and the girl continued to sing, finding her way back to the melody. Her hands clasped the mic tightly, and her body was straight and stiff. The nervousness could also be heard in her voice.

Clara moved forward, encouraging Shay to focus on her. She moved her hands to her diaphragm to signal the singer should take a deep breath. Shay nodded and breathed during a break in the song.

The song came to an end. That's when Clara realized Tucker had left the stage and now stood next to her.

"She has a gift," Clara told him.

"Her mother used to sing in church. She comes by it naturally."

"Do you sing, too?" Clara asked.

From behind them, Avery cleared her throat. Clara spun around in time to see her sister hand Tucker a guitar. "He does sing. And I admit, I brought you both here to trap you into singing."

Clara shook her head at Avery. "Nope. Not me."

Avery pursed her lips in a motherly way that Clara had seen her use on Quinn. "Clara, we need you."

"I'm not even sure if I'll be here."

"The program is two and a half weeks away. You're not leaving before then." Avery appeared set to argue into infinity. She was bullish when it came to getting what she wanted.

What could Clara say? She didn't want to stand on a stage with a growing belly. People would talk. They would gossip. Of course, she'd been the subject of gossip for a big part of her life, and she should be used to it.

Tucker strummed the guitar. "I'm game if you are."

Clara closed her eyes, and then she nodded. "Fine."

Avery clapped her hands and smiled big. "I won."

"You always do," Clara said. "What is it you want us to sing?"

"'What Child Is This?'"

"Do you want us to practice now?" Tucker asked.

Avery grinned. Of course she did.

Clara sighed as she headed for the stage stairs with Tucker close behind. As they went up the steps, Tucker's hand touched her elbow.

It was a wholly unique experience to be treated so carefully. If she'd been anyone else, at any other time, she would have hoped for him to be a part of her life forever. As it was, she could only hope and pray that when it was time to go, she wouldn't miss this man, and his niece, too much.

It was silly, really, because she knew for a fact she would miss them. A lot.

* * *

Tucker could think back to defining moments, things that had changed his life. Having his sister show up on his doorstep with Shay had been one. This moment on stage with Clara might be another.

For a few minutes they'd discussed how to sing the song, when to harmonize and the like. He'd tuned the guitar as she hummed the melody. It had all led up to the moment when they started to sing. It had felt as if something clicked and this is where he was meant to be, and she was the person he was meant to be with. He shook it off because she most definitely was not the woman he'd been waiting for.

She was a shooting star, in his life briefly.

They harmonized during the song's chorus. As Clara sang the last verse, a tear streaked down her cheek. He wanted to swipe it away. He wanted to know what made her cry and why she sometimes seemed so lost in fear.

They sang the final chorus, and she smiled up at him as they ended the song. From across the church, he heard Shay speaking.

"Hi, Mom, it's me, Shay. I just wanted to talk, and I hoped you'd be here soon. Call me back."

Clara looked at him, her eyes reflecting her concern. She had the kind of eyes that revealed every emotion. He nodded and left her there, bounding off the stage to go help.

Before he could reach Shay, she'd dialed again. He got there in time to hear her leaving a second message and to see the look of defeat on her face.

"Mom, I'm in the church Christmas play, and I have a solo. The program is the Wednesday before Christmas if you can be here."

"No answer?" Tucker asked, needlessly. It was obvious from the look on her face that Jana hadn't answered.

"No. She's probably busy with work. Maybe the next time I practice we can record it and send it to her."

"Sure, we can do that." He waited, giving her time to decide what she needed from him.

Tucker didn't know much about kids. He knew about cattle and horses. He knew that with a foal, if he gave it time, it would generally give him a clue as to how it felt about him and what kind of attention it needed. He guessed, or maybe hoped, the same applied in this situation.

He was right. He waited, and suddenly she came at him and put strong kid arms around his waist as she cried. He patted her back and let her cry it out, aware that most of the people around them had moved on to other tasks in order to give them privacy. Except Clara. She waited nearby, and he figured she meant to stay until she knew if Shay needed her. That was the difference between Clara and the housekeepers Shay had run off.

Clara didn't necessarily try to mother Tucker's niece, but she cared. She knew what it was to be a hurting kid. Maybe that had made the difference in his niece: she now had Clara, someone with the shared experience of being a vulnerable teen.

"I'm sorry," Tucker said after a couple of minutes.

"Do you…do you think she's…she's tired of being my mom? If she is, she should give notice." She hiccuped as she spoke, the words coming out in harsh sobs as she continued to cry. "She should give notice. That's…what people do when…they quit a job."

It was painful to hear that this was how Shay felt.

"She isn't going to quit on you," Tucker said. Then he thought about all the things he would say to his sister.

"It's because I'm always in trouble, isn't it?" Shay said after a few minutes.

"It isn't," he insisted.

"I told her I would behave. I told her I wouldn't be a problem."

"Shay, this isn't about you." Clara appeared at his side with a box of tissues. "I'm sorry, I didn't mean to interfere."

"You're not," Tucker assured her. He could use the help.

Clara gave him a watery smile. "When I was a kid, I thought if I was smart enough, if I helped enough, if I didn't eat too much, that my parents would be better. As if my actions would make them turn into responsible adults. It didn't work. My parents were addicts who didn't work, and nothing I said or did would change that. I don't know what is going on with your parents, but I'm fairly sure that it has nothing to do with your behavior. You are a funny, smart kid who I happen to like very much. You can't change their behavior or their choices."

Shay drew in a shuddery breath that nearly broke Tucker's heart. "Thank you."

"I wish I could fix this for you," Tucker told his niece as she moved from his arms, wiping her nose on a second tissue from the box.

"I don't want you to feel stuck with me." Shay looked away as she said the words that completely undid his composure.

"I don't think he feels stuck with you," Clara assured her. "He's your family, and family matters."

He was so angry with his sister right now. Yeah, he

loved her. He also knew he'd forgive her. That didn't mean he wasn't angry. He reminded himself of the verse that said to be angry but not sin. So far, so good. He was just plain old angry.

His sister should be putting her daughter first.

She was thirty-five years old, educated and from a family that would never have treated her the way she was treating her daughter. His parents were good, honest people who had always put their kids first. They were over a thousand miles away and still trying to wrap their minds around the fact that their daughter and son-in-law could do this to their own child.

He patted Shay's back. "I'm sorry. Really sorry. If I could fix this for you, I would."

"I know. It isn't your fault that they're selfish."

He chuckled because she'd hit the nail on the head. "No, it isn't."

"I tried, Uncle Tucker. I tried really hard to be good. I also tried being really bad, thinking that would make her come get me."

"I know," he told her. "Let's just try being you."

"I'll try. But I can't promise anything." She pulled back and swiped at her face. "I'm sorry for the way I've acted, though. I'm also sorry for messing up rehearsals."

Clara nodded toward the stage. "They're finishing up now."

Tucker needed to change the subject. "Hey, the ice rink will be done tomorrow. What do you think about inviting friends over this weekend, and we can have a trial run? I'll build a bonfire and we can roast marshmallows."

"I can bring friends?" Shay asked, her eyes clearing up, and her smile returning. "Can Clara come with us?"

They both looked to Clara. She was shaking her head. "I won't be able to go, but I'm sure you'll have a great time."

Shay started to argue, but he stopped her with a warning look. If Clara didn't want to go, he was sure she had a good reason.

He was actually relieved she'd rejected the invitation. The less time he spent with Clara, the better. He might be older and wiser than his lovesick seventeen-year-old self who had lost his heart to a girl named Junie. But he also knew that if he spent too much time with Clara, he'd want more time with her and not less. She was a dangerous combination of smart, witty and vulnerable.

His best plan of action was to focus on Shay and to keep Clara firmly in a place of friendship.

Chapter Eight

Clara pulled the last towel out of the dryer and folded it in thirds and then thirds again, the way she'd found the towels in the guest bathroom of Tucker's home. It was Tuesday, and he'd left her alone to go work cattle. She'd been making her way down the list he'd left, a list that had started with taking Shay to school that morning.

Oh, first she'd made a breakfast of not-quite-burnt scrambled eggs and almost-crispy microwave bacon. Shay had laughed at the bacon because anyone should be able to make microwave bacon.

She carried the towels to the bathroom at the far end of the hall on the main level of the split-level house. Tucker said it had belonged to his grandparents. They'd built in the 1960s after the original farmhouse had been deemed not worth remodeling. He'd replaced the dark paneled walls with drywall and the carpeting with hardwood floors.

It was a lovely house, not modern or fancy but comfortable with big rooms, a lot of windows and a covered porch where a person could sit and have a cup of coffee, possibly catching sight of deer as they crossed the field to graze.

As Clara stacked the towels in the bathroom closet, her phone rang. She finished and pulled her phone out of her pocket, surprised that Avery would be calling. She answered, knowing she wouldn't like how this call went.

"Clara, I'm sorry to bother you but Nan is having some…" There was a heavy pause. "She's in trouble."

"What happened?"

"She's at a store in Pickens. I'm not sure why she went there. The cashier said she showed up about an hour ago and seemed confused. She filled her cart with diapers and baby food, and then she continued to circle the store. After a while she seemed to realize what she'd put in her cart, and she became distraught. She knows who she is, but she told the workers that she doesn't know what she's doing there or how to get home."

"I'll go get her. What about her car?" Clara left the laundry basket on the kitchen table, grabbed her purse off the counter and ran for the back door.

"We're going to have her car towed to her house. I'm sorry that you have to do this—"

"Stop," Clara interrupted. "I'm here, and I'm going to help."

On the patio, she stopped and made quick eye contact with Tucker. How long had he been standing there?

Avery said, "I know, but I didn't want to bother you. I would go, but I'm at work. And Grayson is on a job site in Springfield."

"Tucker won't mind if I leave." She looked at him, and he nodded. "I'll call you as soon as I can."

"What happened?" Tucker asked as he walked next to her.

"Nan is in Pickens. I need to go get her. I'm sorry. I know I have a job and—"

"You don't have to apologize. And you don't have to do this alone," he said. "I'm going with you. Give me your keys and I'll drive."

"You don't have to do that," she argued, but she didn't put up much of a fight. She didn't want to do this alone. "I can drive myself."

"I'm driving you."

She handed him her keys. "Thank you."

"I'm sorry about this," Tucker told her as they pulled onto the road.

Clara nodded. She'd been praying, for Nan, for all of them, because the future was full of unknowns. Her pregnancy, Nan's dementia, Shay and her parents.

"I wonder how people navigate life without faith," she said. "Everything comes at us so quickly, and we never know when things might change unexpectedly."

"I can't imagine life without faith, so I'm not sure how they do it."

"Nan has always taken care of all of us," Clara said, comforted by his strong hand that had reached for hers. "She'll be devastated when it comes time for her to be taken care of."

He smiled at that. "She has a stubborn streak that's wider than the James River, but we'll all be here for her, and for you all."

Suddenly tears welled in her eyes, and if she opened her mouth, she'd cry. She was glad he'd offered to come with her. It wasn't easy, opening this door to him, but she'd never been more relieved to have someone in her life, someone to lean on. Even if it was just temporary, even if it was just for a season, she knew she had a friend she could count on.

The drive to Pickens didn't take long. There wasn't near enough time to talk herself into being brave. Brave for herself and for Nan. A long time ago, she'd lived in this town. Then she'd spent the last fifteen years avoiding it. Her parents' house had been a ramshackle place with holes in the roof, boarded-up windows and a front porch with a partially caved-in deck.

She tamped down the fear that she might meet one of her parents here in town, in the store where Nan had lost track of who she was and where she belonged. She wouldn't get caught up in her past when Nan seemed to be forgetting her present.

Tucker parked in front of the store. He gave her a careful look. "Are you okay?"

She drew in a deep breath. "I'm okay. And thank you for coming with me. I'm glad you're here."

He winked. "Me, too."

Together they walked through the sliding-glass doors of the store. Together they saw Nan sitting on a chair behind the counter, a police officer sitting close to her, chatting and laughing as Nan told him a story. Nan saw her and cried out.

"Clara, what in the world are you doing here?" Nan said as she tossed a bottle of soda in the trash. Nan never drank soda.

"I came to give you a ride home," Clara said as she pasted on a smile and closed the distance between them, Tucker close behind.

"Well, why would you do that? My car is right out front."

Clara didn't know what to say. Nan stood before

her, obviously more lucid now. She seemed to be having a good time visiting with her new friends. The real evidence of her confusion lay in the grocery cart filled with baby items. Diapers, wipes, food, infant-size sleepers. Why? Clara's hand immediately went to her belly. Surely Nan wasn't purchasing these things for her? Tucker gave her a questioning look. He'd connected the dots as well.

Nan also looked at the cart, and the second her gaze landed on the items, she looked lost. Worse than lost: she looked devastated.

"I forgot," Nan said. "I forgot that he's gone."

"He?"

The police officer quickly shook his head, but it was too late. Nan reached into the cart and pulled out a tiny sleeper. "My baby boy."

Clara wanted to correct her foster mom. But the look of devastation on Nan's face stopped Clara.

"Nan, we should go." Clara moved the cart aside. "If we need anything, we'll come back later."

"Are you driving?" Nan asked, her tone full of forced cheerfulness.

"Yes, I'm driving. Don't worry, I'm much better than I was fourteen years ago."

They both laughed, but the laughter sounded hollow.

"What do we owe you good folks?" Nan asked. "Did I make any messes?"

The cashier patted Nan's arm. "We loved visiting with you, Miss Nan."

Nan put a hand over the other woman's hand. "Honey, you've been real sweet to me. I hope I can come back again sometime." She turned to the deputy.

"And you, young man, you stay safe. Thank you for sitting with me."

"It was my pleasure, Miss Nan."

The police officer walked them to Clara's car. He helped Nan in, waited until her seat belt was buckled and then gently closed the door.

"You've got this." Tucker touched his hand to hers as he gave the reassurance. "I'll be right behind you in Nan's car."

She nodded, afraid if she spoke, the tears would break free. Tucker seemed to understand and he remained silent as he walked her to the driver's side of the car. He opened the door, hesitating a little as if he might say something. Instead he leaned in, kissed her cheek, then waited as she got behind the wheel so he could close the door.

As they drove away, a tear trickled down Nan's cheek. She didn't move to wipe it away. Clara's breath caught at the fear, the hurt on Nan's face. What could she say that would make sense? She couldn't tell Nan that everything would be okay. She couldn't say that this would pass. The truth was, this would hurt. They were all going to feel the pain of slowly watching this woman they loved slip away from them.

"I drove to the store," Nan said. "I guess I got lost along the way, and then when I got there and started shopping, I couldn't figure out why I was there."

Clara found herself wishing for Tucker's presence because she needed someone. She wanted to tell him she was frightened for this woman. She was frightened for their future and for things she couldn't control, both past and present.

A short time ago she'd told him she didn't know how

people handled their lives without faith. She had faith. She also knew the faith wouldn't make all of this disappear, but it would give her strength.

The direction her thoughts had taken frightened her. She'd never wanted so much to talk to one person. One specific person. If she had, the person had always been Nan.

"We're more than conquerors, Nan," she whispered, because they were the words Nan would have said to her.

Nan reached for her hand. Their fingers laced together, Nan's were thin, cool, strong. Clara wanted to give Nan her warmth, to hold on and keep her strong.

"The baby food was for Ryan," Nan said after a few minutes.

The words jerked Clara from her own thoughts. She glanced at Nan. "Ryan?"

"I had a baby once, a long time ago. A sweet little boy. I was eighteen, and my fiancé had gone to war. We…we anticipated our vows, and when he left, I was pregnant. He never knew about the baby, and since he never came back…"

Clara reached out, and Nan's hand slid back into hers. "Oh, Nan."

"I was sent to live with a cousin, and she adopted my little baby boy. Ryan. I stayed the summer, and there were times when I'd sit up all night and rock him, knowing that I'd never hold another baby. Word had come that Jacob died in battle. He was the only man I ever loved."

Clara gave Nan's hand a squeeze.

Nan sniffled. "It was a long time ago, and I rarely think about either of them. Ryan grew up to be a lawyer. He lives in Colorado. I doubt they ever told him about me, and I never tried to contact him."

"Maybe you should," Clara suggested. "He's a grown man, and I'm sure he'd like to know you."

"Oh, I don't know. I think it's best to let him live his own life. I'll forget him soon enough."

"I don't think you will," Clara said. "You were thinking of him today."

Nan smiled at that. "I know. For a few minutes I was that young girl again. I thought I needed to take care of my child. Isn't that silly, how the brain works?"

Clara remained silent because she knew that opening her mouth to speak would be like turning a valve and releasing the tears she was barely managing to hold back. She wondered how much of her own situation had triggered Nan's trip into the past.

"Don't cry for me," Nan scolded. "I'm going to be okay, and so are you. You're going to face whatever happened in St. Louis, and maybe eventually you'll talk about it."

"I will," she whispered. She would keep the promise, but today wasn't the day to share. Today was about Nan, and Clara needed her thoughts focused on her foster mother.

"Oh, Clara girl, you've always been my most stubborn secret keeper. Even Regan knows how to open up from time to time."

Regan had been older when she first came to Nan's. Almost sixteen, a little wild and headstrong, unwilling to talk to the others. She was now a lawyer in Kansas City.

"How is Regan?"

"Oh, I'd say she's doing okay. She's busy with her career, and I worry she's burning the candle on both ends."

"She's always been driven," Clara agreed. Her foster sister had been a bit dark, back in the day, and very studious.

"Yes," Nan agreed. "Regan is driven. She hides a lot of herself."

"I know she does. We're here," Clara announced, as they pulled up to Nan's white-sided farmhouse. Sugar the collie was there to greet them.

Nan looked out the window and slowly exhaled. "Yes, here we are. I need you to make a book, a memory book. Would you do that for me? I'll tell you my stories, and you write them down. I don't want them to disappear, Clara."

"I'll help you." The words came out on a sob that she couldn't quite hide. The idea of Nan forgetting bruised her heart.

"It'll be okay," Nan assured her. "I have hope, Clara. And I pray every day that my girls will be my legacy and continue that hope."

"We will," Clara promised.

As they were crossing the yard, Avery pulled into the driveway. She jumped out of her car and hurried toward them. Nan sighed.

"There she is, the worrier," Nan said, with a smile that dissolved into a sadness that Clara had rarely seen on the older woman's face.

Clara gave Avery a quick, warning look. A hand slid into hers, big and strong. Tucker's hand. He stood next to her, a towering giant of a man. A man who made her want things. She wanted to redo the past, to make herself a better person, a person that a man like Tucker would want in his life. A woman who wasn't struggling to make decisions that would change everything.

"You made it home okay," Avery said as she joined them, keeping her tone light.

"We did. I can't see a reason for all the fuss." Nan pushed the front door open and headed for the kitchen. "I need lunch. Are you two girls hungry?"

"Not really." Clara glanced at her watch.

"Do you need to go?" Nan asked. "I know you're both working today. Don't stay here hovering and worrying. I can take care of myself."

"We know you can," Avery reassured their foster mom.

Nan sat down at the table. "I'm going to tell you both something, and then you have to go, Clara. I know that you need get back to Tucker's to help with…" Nan hesitated and then shook her head "…the girl."

"Shay," Avery reminded gently.

"Yes, Shay." Nan brightened. "Before the two of you leave, I need to tell you something. This farm and my business are in a trust. I named Grayson as executor. I took care of this last year because I didn't want anyone questioning if I was in my right mind. I left the house to Emery, because I know the two of you have other options and Emery loves this old place. I'll split the land between you girls, the ones who have continued to make Pleasant your home."

"Nan, don't…" Clara wanted to put her hands over her ears. Nan was meant to live forever, watching over her flock of girls, keeping them all safe and heading in the right direction.

"I can't stop it, Clara. Life catches up with all of us. And this stuff…it has to be dealt with."

Avery sat down at the table. "Okay, tell us what you need from us."

Nan's eyes filled with tears, and she smiled up at Clara. "Don't worry, I won't be leaving you for a long time yet."

Clara leaned to kiss Nan's cheek. "I love you."

"I love you more."

Clara sat down to listen as Nan talked.

A short time later, Clara and Tucker crossed the yard to her car.

"I'm sorry," Tucker said as he opened the passenger door of her car.

"Me, too," she answered, looking up at him before getting in.

He caressed her cheek, a comforting gesture that had her closing her eyes, wanting to lean in to him. She held herself back, because if she leaned, she'd never want to walk away. Tucker deserved better. She wasn't going to let herself get tangled up in something that was temporary.

"We should go," she whispered, her eyes still closed.

He kissed the top of her head, and then he was gone. She opened her eyes, watching as he rounded her car to get in on the driver's side. In all of her adult life, she'd never felt this before, this need to be in someone else's life.

It was a dangerous thought, one that she couldn't allow to take root. No matter how good it felt.

Tucker parked her car in the driveway outside his garage. She'd been silent the whole way home, and now she silently got out of the vehicle.

He'd been tempted to kiss her, back at Nan's. In comfort, he had told himself. It had been more than that, though. He wasn't a man prone to lying, so he wasn't going to lie to himself. He liked Clara. He liked her a lot.

"What's Grayson doing here?" she asked, looking in the direction of the barn.

He hadn't noticed before, but Grayson's truck was parked near the barn, and Grayson was riding a big roan around the arena.

"My new horse. I'd forgotten that he planned to bring him today." Tucker stopped to watch the horse and rider as they moved in figure eights. The horse was nice, real nice. Grayson had guaranteed he'd like the animal. They were planning on team roping come spring.

"Let's go meet him," Clara said. "I need the distraction."

But she hesitated, her hand going to her belly.

"Are you okay?"

She grimaced, then attempted a smile.

"Of course I am."

Grayson spotted them and rode the horse up to the fence.

"Hey! How's Nan?" he asked as he swung his right leg over the horse's back and dropped to the ground.

"Good as can be expected," Tucker answered.

Grayson walked to the gate with the horse. "Are you going to ride him?"

Tucker shrugged. "Yeah, I'll try him out."

He slipped through the gate, taking the reins from his partner. He checked the saddle, adjusted the stirrups and mounted. The horse took a step back, unsure of the new rider.

Tucker spoke to him, giving him a minute to adjust.

He was a big animal, the kind of horse Tucker liked. The kind that didn't feel like a pony to a man well over six feet tall. He rode the horse around the arena, letting him open up into a nice lope. He had a good gait, smooth and easy. He started to say something to Grayson, but he noticed Clara had disappeared.

He rode up to the gate. "Where'd she go?"

"Inside. She said she had to start dinner before she leaves for the day."

Tucker swung his leg over the horse's back and landed on the ground next to him. The horse turned to push at his arm with a soft nudge.

"Are you going to finish up?" Grayson asked from the gate.

"I'm finished." He led the horse from the arena. "You're going to make me a decent cow horse."

He patted the animal's red-brown neck.

"Talking to the horse?" Grayson asked with a grin.

"Yeah, the horse is decent company. You, not so much," Tucker said, almost smiling. "I'll take him. Will you put him in a stall for me?"

"Am I your ranch hand now?" Grayson asked.

"No, but you're my friend, and Clara shouldn't be alone."

Grayson gave him a long look. "What about you? Are you going to be okay when she leaves? She's never been one to stay in one place for very long."

"I'll be fine."

Grayson shrugged and took the reins.

"I'll take care of the horse. You take care of Clara."

Tucker didn't give him a chance to say more. Grayson liked to give advice, to get in other people's business. Tucker wasn't in the mood for his interference.

He found her in the kitchen, stirring hamburger in a skillet. For a minute he watched her, then he turned off the burner and took the spatula from her hand.

"I'm busy," she told him.

"I know. You're busy trying to pretend everything is okay."

"I'm making a tater tot casserole. Nan said that even I couldn't mess that up." She choked on a sob. "I can't do this."

"You can. You're stronger than you think. Nan is going to be okay."

She shook her head at him. "No! No, she isn't going to be okay. And I don't know if I'm ever going to be okay again."

He couldn't argue with her because he didn't know her story or how she felt. There was nothing worse than being told how to feel.

"Do you want to talk?" he offered as he started a pot of coffee.

She watched, leaning against the counter as he scooped coffee into the filter. He pretended he was focused on the task and that he wasn't tempted to pull her close. She needed to be held, but her body language said maybe she wouldn't welcome a hug.

"It's going to be so difficult, watching her slip away from us," Clara said. "And how do I leave here, knowing this is happening? How do I leave her? When I came home, I thought it would be easy. I'd come here, get my life together, work through some decisions I have to make, then I would go away again."

"There are no easy answers," he said.

"Why is it things always happen this way?" she

asked, raising liquid brown eyes to his, her expression imploring.

"Things like this?"

Her hand had gone to her belly, whether intentionally or out of habit. He waited, knowing she needed to unburden herself. A heaviness stole over him because he knew that her story wouldn't be easy to hear.

"Like Nan," she started with the obvious. "Like this baby."

She didn't cry. She appeared stronger than ever, clear eyes, chin up.

"You're strong." The words slipped out, and she shook her head, denying them.

"I'm not strong," she said. "I'm afraid."

"You can be strong, brave even, and still be afraid."

"I hope you're right. There's a lot coming at me, and I'd welcome some bravery right now. I don't know how to watch Nan slip away from us. I don't know how to help her."

"I think Nan will let you know what she needs."

"You're right."

She'd let her gaze drift down, to the hand covering her belly.

"I'm here," he assured her. "If you need someone. If you need to talk."

"That's a big offer," she told him.

"It's one that I don't give lightly. I mean it. If you are in trouble, if you need help, whatever it is, I'm here."

"I was attacked in the parking garage near the hotel I managed. By one of my employees."

The admission took him by surprise, nearly knocking the breath from him.

Rage and protectiveness coursed through him. He

closed the distance between them and gathered her close, holding her as she fought tears.

"I'm pregnant with the child of the man who broke into the back of my car." Her voice broke, and he felt her tears against his chest. "I can't look in the rearview mirror of my car without seeing him there. I know he isn't there, but I see him. Every single time I get in my car, I see him. I remember. And when I think of this baby, I don't know what to do. I don't know how I could hold or comfort them when I fear looking into their eyes will be the same as looking in my rearview mirror."

He had no words for that kind of anguish. He couldn't tell her she would love her baby. He couldn't assure her that it would be okay. No one could say those words to her.

"I'm here," he promised, whispering the words against the honey-scented curls. The words were a big promise from a man who knew better. She wasn't his to hold or to protect. He couldn't change any of this for her. He couldn't undo what had happened.

"I haven't told anyone," she whispered as she pulled away from him, reaching for a napkin to wipe her eyes. "I haven't told them about the attack. I haven't told them about the baby, although I think that part is pretty obvious. And no one asks, because I think they're afraid of what I'll tell them."

She'd held this all in, not sharing with anyone. Not Nan or Avery, the people closest to her, the ones she should have told.

She'd trusted him with her story and her pain. Memories of sixteen-year-old Junie slipped in to taunt him. He'd been a naive teenager, sadly unequipped to deal with Junie's problems.

Fifteen years later, did he know more now than he had then?

Moving away from him, she gave him her back as she wiped her eyes and then pretended to concentrate on the ground meat in the skillet, turning on the burner and stirring it with the spatula. After it was done browning, she spooned it out onto a paper towel. He remained where she'd left him, watching as she mixed frozen tater tots, cream of mushroom soup and the cooked ground meat.

She spread it into a baking dish.

"I'll bake this before I leave today," she told him without looking up. She covered it in foil and placed it in the fridge.

"I can bake it," he offered.

She faced him with a fire in her brown eyes that took him by surprise.

"I don't need to be coddled," she informed him with a tilt of her chin. "I'm not going to fall apart. I shared something with you. It just…came out. But it wasn't an invitation for you to become my protective older brother. Brothers do not hug like that."

At that, he grinned. He shouldn't have, but he couldn't stop himself.

"Stop smiling at me that way," she demanded as the corner of her mouth tugged upward. "It isn't funny."

And then she giggled a little, swiping at a few remaining tears as she did. "I'm unhinged."

"You're not," he told her. "You're brave and strong, and I can assure you I'm not your brother. I can bake this casserole because I have nothing else to do."

"And because you think I'm at the end of my rope."

"Never," he said. "I think you're hanging onto a lifeline, and God is right there with you. You're not at the end of your rope."

"You're right," she said. "It's obviously the hormones. I'm crying one minute and laughing the next. It even affects how I feel about the pregnancy. A few times in the same day, I can change my mind about this tiny person growing inside me."

"You'll make the right decisions."

"I've already decided. I called an adoption agency."

He remained silent for a moment, needing time to think. He poured himself a cup of coffee, then held up the pot to her. She shook her head.

"It's a selfish decision, isn't it?" she asked. "I mean, that is why you're not saying anything, isn't it?" She kept talking, as if desperate to fill the silence. "I didn't make this decision lightly. I'm doing what I think is best for the baby and for myself."

"Shh," he finally said. "No one can tell you that your decision is wrong. I obviously don't know how you feel or what you've been through. What I don't understand is…" he hesitated, because he didn't really have the right to step into her life "…why haven't you told Nan or Avery about this?"

"I don't know. It's been hard to discuss it, and I also don't want them to be upset with me." She gave him a shy, half smile. "I don't know why I told you. I guess you caught me in a moment of weakness."

"For what it's worth, I know it can't be easy. I mean, I'm obviously a man, so…"

She grinned at that and the mood lightened. "You are a man. But not a brother."

He felt unfamiliar heat crawl up his face. "Right, I'm a man."

Her humor vanished, but the thread connecting them tightened, creating an emotional bond he hadn't expected.

"I'm dealing with a lot of what-ifs, Tucker. What if I can't love this baby? What if I am always afraid, always feeling this sense of dread and panic? I'm trying to find peace in God, and every day I wake up, thanking Him that I'm alive. Faith doesn't mean that I'm instantly healed, as if it didn't happen. Faith doesn't mean that I can keep this baby."

Tucker was silent, not sure what he could say.

"Tucker, I…" She stopped, then she smiled sweetly. "Thank you. For listening. Thank you for not judging. Or at least, for not saying it out loud."

She'd planned to say more. He wanted to know what she'd planned to say because it had been about him, about her, about them. He knew it beyond a shadow of a doubt. It had been there in her eyes.

"You need someone in your court."

"And you're going to be that someone?" she teased.

His phone rang.

"Saved by the bell," she told him. "Go take care of business. I promise, I'm okay. I have moments when I think I might fall apart, but I never do. Or at least not for long."

She stood on tiptoes and kissed his cheek.

He took her advice and escaped.

Chapter Nine

Friday evening, Clara stood alongside Nan, Avery, Grayson and Quinn, stunned by the brilliance of twinkling lights that decorated the Riverside Campground and Outfitters. Lights had been wrapped around the bare tree limbs, strung on wires high above their heads and along the barrier that surrounded the ice rink. Several bonfires had been built, and Tucker was providing s'more-making kits for the skaters.

The concession stand served snacks as well as warm drinks. Heaters warmed the pavilion area where people could sit at picnic tables.

"This is amazing," Quinn said as she twirled around, staring up at lights. "Where do we get our skates?"

"At the pavilion," Grayson said. He held Avery's hand, but his free hand went to Quinn's shoulder. "Straight ahead. Go find your size."

"Awesome. Thanks, Dad." Quinn hurried away.

"This is so lovely," Nan said. "What a nice thing for our little town."

"Very nice," Clara agreed as she walked next to Nan.

Grayson and Avery walked on ahead, joining their

daughter at the pavilion where others were paying for skates and then sitting on benches near the rink and lacing up. Tucker was there with Shay.

Quinn had found Shay, and now the younger girls huddled up together, all smiles and giggles. Tucker shared something with Grayson, and the two men laughed at whatever he'd said.

Clara's heart ached because she wanted those moments of lightness and laughter to be her normal once again. She'd gotten so caught up in the darkness, in the memories, that she'd felt it weighing down on her heart, changing her. She didn't want to lose herself.

"You're drifting again," Nan said as she leaned in close, holding onto Clara's arm.

"I'm sorry."

They were nearing the pavilion. Tucker glanced their way, and his expression became unreadable. Age-old insecurities cropped up, making her question her friendship with this man.

"Will you skate?" she asked Nan in an effort to distract herself.

"I think I'm going to sit here where it's warm," Nan said. "I'll have some hot wassail and one of those deep-fried cookies."

"Do you want me to get it for you?"

Nan waved a hand. "Of course not. I can get it when I'm ready. Don't hover over me and worry yourself sick."

"I wouldn't dream of it," she denied.

Nan gave her a censoring look. "You would."

"Clara, are you going to skate?" Shay hobbled in her direction, already wearing skates.

"I don't think so," Clara said. "I've only been on

skates a few times, and I haven't really mastered the skill."

"I'll take you around the rink," a masculine voice said from behind her.

She spun around to face him, and a wave of dizziness hit her. If she couldn't turn without falling, she definitely couldn't ice-skate. Tucker's hand shot out, grabbing her arm when she wobbled.

"Are you okay?" his voice rumbled near her ear.

"Yes, I'm good."

"Do you want to skate?"

"Please skate with us, Clara." Shay grabbed her hand. Quinn jumped in also. Both girls begging her to join them on the ice.

"I don't know if I should." She looked to Avery who was standing behind Quinn and who had most likely guessed her condition. Not that it hadn't become painfully obvious to anyone who cared to take notice. She was in her second trimester.

"I think if you're careful and if you have someone to hold onto," Avery said with a wink.

Clara blushed and mouthed, "Later," to her foster sister when no one was watching.

Avery laughed, not at all chastised.

"All right, then, let's get you some skates," Tucker offered, ignoring the back-and-forth between Clara and Avery.

"Yes, let's."

A few moments later, she was pulling on her skates. Tucker sat down next to her and did up his own.

He stood and held out a hand. She hesitated briefly before sliding her hand into his and allowing him to pull her to her feet. Quinn, Shay, Avery and Grayson had all disappeared. There were people all around them. And yet, it seemed as if they were all alone.

With his hand wrapped around her elbow, he guided her to the rink. Christmas lights twinkled all around them. In addition to the lights in the trees and around the rink, there were shapes made with wire and frames. A Christmas tree, an ornament, a nativity scene, complete with sheep, donkey and camels, all glittering with clear lights.

They stopped at the rink's edge.

"Ready?" Tucker asked her.

"Ready as I'll ever be. Don't let me fall."

"I won't let you fall," he said. The promise seemed deeper than the moment, as if it meant more. She couldn't allow that. She couldn't overthink everything he said.

Avery and Grayson skated past, contented smiles on their faces, his arm around Avery's waist.

"They're a good couple," Clara said.

"They are. They've found each other, the way they were meant to."

"Is that what you think, that they were meant to be together?"

"You don't?"

"I don't know what I think anymore. I haven't dated a lot, and these past few months have made me question everything. One moment took my sense of self and security. One moment changed everything. Was that also meant to be? I... Sorry. Let's just skate."

"I believe in *meant to be*," he said, his voice heavy with emotion. "But what happened to you was..." He shook his head. "You're right, we should skate."

She knew what he meant, and she was glad to let the conversation go.

Tucker slipped an arm around her waist and swept her onto the ice. "May I put my arm around you?" he asked.

"If that means I won't fall and break something, please do." But she wanted more than the safety of his arm around her. She wanted his touch, his strength and the way he made her feel whole.

The thought frightened her, but she couldn't make herself pull away.

His arm went around her waist, and he eased them forward, skating with the finesse of someone who had skated often. The cool night air brushed their faces as lights twinkled in the dark December night. As they circled the rink, Christmas songs drifted around them. It was beautiful and peaceful, and Clara thought if she hadn't been cold, she might have stayed there for hours.

"Trust me?" Tucker asked as they skated a second lap around the rink.

Trust him? It was a loaded question. Trust him with her heart? Her emotions? Or skating? He arched a brow, as if knowing the direction of her thoughts.

"I know you won't let me fall," she answered.

He moved so that he was skating backward. He held both of her hands, smiling as he weaved their way through the other skaters. She felt free and happy and so many other things, the emotions coming at her like a spring storm that would either bring rain and flowers or destruction.

He spun back around, and she was suddenly at his side again, his arm around her waist.

A little boy skated past them, his legs quavering as

he tried to find purchase on the ice. Tucker swerved to miss him.

Clara tripped, nearly falling, but Tucker caught her against him, pulling her back against his chest as he guided her to the edge of the rink.

"Are you all right?" he asked, breathing close to her ear, a tremor of panic in his voice.

"I am, but I would be even better if you didn't sound frightened."

"I'm sorry," he said, still holding her.

His arms were around her. There were twinkling lights, Christmas music and people skating past. And feelings. So many feelings she couldn't untangle them all.

Tucker held Clara in his arms. She was soft and sweet and staring up at him with those soulful brown eyes. The words *meant to be* were teasing him as he held her close. Those were words he needed to fight off, feelings he needed to push away. At the moment, holding her the way he was, he couldn't convince himself to let her go.

She would be gone soon enough.

"You're sure you are okay?" he asked again as he held her close, afraid to let her go. Afraid he couldn't let her go.

"I'm fine. Is he okay? The little boy?"

Tucker had forgotten the child. He glanced back and saw that the boy was up, smiling and holding the hand of a man who seemed to be his father. "I think he's fine."

"I think I'm done skating," she said softly, his gaze lingering on her as she said the words.

Instead of coming to his senses, he did the unimagi-

nable. He scooped her off her feet and carried her off
the ice and away from the rink, stopping to grab her
shoes and putting the fuzzy boots on her belly before
continuing on to a bonfire that hadn't yet been claimed.

If someone asked him what he was doing, he'd have
to come up with a reasonable answer. She'd almost been
hurt out there on the ice. The incident had shaken him.
He'd been concerned for her safety.

He'd needed to hold her. The thought nearly brought
a groan from him. She was not his. She was a woman
passing through, helping him with Shay, undoing his
sensible and well-planned-out life.

He didn't do impulsive things. He'd spent six months
researching the truck he'd recently bought. He'd planned
his campground and river-outfitter business for ten
years before breaking ground. Shay being dropped in
his life had been unsettling. Clara was downright mind-
boggling.

"What are you doing?" she asked, looking around,
as if seeking an escape. Even she seemed to know that
this was out of the ordinary for him.

"I'm making sure you're okay. If you want me to put
you down, I will."

There was a moment's hesitation, but then she nodded, trusting him. Her trust was not something he would
take for granted. He cherished it as he carried her away
from the crowds, from questioning looks, from Avery.
Grayson held his wife's hand as she tried to skate toward
the exit. Tucker saw their quick exchange of words and
then watched as Avery skated away with her husband.

The warmth of the bonfire was welcome as he settled
Clara on a bench. She shivered slightly, and he reached
for her hands, holding them in his, warming them.

"What are we doing here?" she asked.

"I'm going to take off your skates," he answered.

"I can do that myself."

"I know you can." He removed one skate, set it aside and rubbed her foot before sliding on the boot she handed him. He did the other skate and then the remaining boot. He watched as she flinched and her hand went to her belly.

"Are you all right?" he asked.

"I think I am." She started to stand, but he took her hand and helped her to her feet.

"You think?"

She stood before him, her hand still resting on the belly that was just now beginning to show evidence of the life growing inside her. She drew in a breath and exhaled, her features relaxing.

"Yes, I'm fine. I think it was just the adrenaline of nearly falling over the little boy."

"I wouldn't have let you fall," he assured her.

"I know," she said softly. "I should go check on Nan."

"I'll walk with you."

She smiled up at him, her brown eyes reflecting the twinkle of Christmas lights, her cheeks rosy from the cold and the exertion of skating. "You need to get your shoes."

He hesitated, wanting to ignore the obvious. She was right. He should walk away. He should get his shoes, take off the skates and take care of his business. Instead, he touched her hand, stopping her from running away.

"Tucker?" She looked up at him, unsure, as if she knew the direction his thoughts had taken.

"I'd like to kiss you."

He expected to be told to jump in the river. Instead, she touched his cheek and whispered, "I'm afraid."

"So am I."

"But I'd like it, if you'd kiss me."

He drew her close and brushed his lips against hers, noticing she tasted like mint and chocolate. She was familiar and unknown, all at the same time. A song played on the speakers, one about winter love and gifts that last a lifetime, a kiss on a cold December day.

Meant to be. The words hung between them as his lips claimed hers. She let him kiss her once, twice. Her hands were on his shoulders, and he wanted to hold her longer, maybe forever. It was a crazy thought.

"Thank you," she said as she pulled away.

"Those aren't the words I expected," he told her, still reeling with his own unexpected feelings. Feelings he knew would chase her away if he shared them.

"Thank you for showing me that I can be held or kissed and I won't fall apart. I have this friend, Clyde." She smiled at him, and he imagined the look on his face showed his shock. "Clyde is what I call my anxiety. Sometimes it feels as if there is an elephant sitting on me, and I can't take a deep breath. I thought if I gave it a name, it wouldn't have such a hold over me."

"I helped you overcome Clyde?" he asked.

"Yes, you did." She gave his hand a squeeze. "I didn't mean to use you."

"Use me?" He was confused.

"The kiss," she explained. "I wanted to be kissed by someone I trust, someone gentle and kind."

"I'm not sure if that is a resounding compliment or not." Once again, he was the good guy, the friend.

"I didn't mean it like that," she said, her eyes filling

with regret. "I wanted you to kiss me, Tucker. I wanted to be held by you."

"Sure, as an experiment." His feelings were hurt. He was a grown man, and he hadn't expected to feel this way.

"No," she denied.

Whatever else she planned to say was cut short.

"There you are!" Shay hurried toward them, Quinn right behind her. Both girls carried the fixings for s'mores and roasting sticks.

"Here we are," Clara said with a too-bright smile.

Shay's focus darted from Clara to Tucker. Her eyes narrowed, but she didn't say whatever she'd been meaning to. Lips pursed, she glared at him.

"Are you girls having fun?" Clara asked as she reclaimed the chair in the circle of the fire's warmth.

"We are," Quinn said, obviously unaware of the tension. "My dad is getting funnel cakes. Mom said she would get drinks. This is so much fun, Tucker!"

"Funnel cakes and s'mores. That won't be a sugar rush," Tucker joked. His attention returned to Clara. There was a tightness around her mouth that worried him.

As the girls scooted close to the fire to roast marshmallows, he claimed the chair next to hers.

"What's wrong?" he said.

"Please. Let it go. Avery and Grayson are heading this way with Nan. We can talk about this later. Right now, I'd love nothing more than a s'more."

Tucker pulled off his cowboy hat and ran a hand through his hair. She wasn't going to talk to him now, but he had a suspicion there was more to this than simply a kiss. Unfortunately, the others had arrived, and Clara was on her feet.

Clara motioned for Nan to sit down. "Should I get s'more kits for the rest of you?"

"I would love one," Nan said as she settled in a chair near the fire.

Tucker started to say something, to stop Clara from leaving. He considered telling her he'd go get them. But he had a pretty good idea that if he did any of those things, she'd make sure he knew that one kiss didn't give him any rights. To know her thoughts, to tell her what to do or even to feel that there might be more kisses to come.

Meant to be.

Those were three words he needed to not connect to Clara Fisher.

Easier said than done.

Chapter Ten

The best plan of action, Clara thought, would be to escape church without speaking to Tucker Church. The plan had been hatched while sitting through the service, watching as he came forward to lead the worship music in the absence of the music minister. Singing songs about faith and the greatness of God with a guitar in his hands was one of the most alluring things she'd ever witnessed. It made Tucker genuine and real. It made him even more attractive, if that was possible.

Tucker wasn't a charmer. He didn't set out to win hearts. He was kind, giving and disarming.

He'd let her share her secrets, her fears, and he'd made her feel safe. Then he'd kissed her.

That kiss had changed everything. First, it had made her realize that she wasn't completely broken. Also, it had made her completely aware that Tucker Church might possibly be the kind of man that every girl should dream of. It had also made it almost impossible to look at him, because if she did she might reveal all of these emotions she was trying very hard to deny.

After the closing prayer, as everyone stood to say

their goodbyes, Clara hurried out. Unfortunately, Avery met her at the back door and stopped her from leaving.

"Where are you going?" Avery asked.

"Oh, hi. I was just heading to my car. I thought you were with the youth group."

"I was, but we're finished." Avery arched a brow. "Why are you in such a rush to get out of here?"

"We have things to do, remember? Nan and I are preparing meals today. For the seniors."

Avery's expression brightened. "Right, I'd forgotten. That works out perfectly, though."

"How?"

"Don't sound so upset about it," Avery teased. "The teens are caroling today. We can meet up and make it a bigger event. Food and caroling. The residents will love it."

Clara didn't know what to say and didn't get a chance. Quinn ran through the doors, out of breath and upset. She spotted the two of them and hurried to her mother.

"Mom, Shay is really upset."

"I need you to start at the beginning and give me all of the details, Quinn."

As she spoke, Avery motioned for Tucker. He'd just finished unplugging the guitar from the amp and he was talking to the pastor. When he saw Avery with Quinn, worry flashed across his face. He said something to the other man before heading their way.

"What's up?" he asked as he approached.

"Shay got a phone call from her mom, and she was really upset," Quinn told him. "She took off down by the creek."

"By the creek?" Tucker repeated, and when Quinn nodded, he ran out the door.

Avery started to say something, but Clara didn't wait to hear what. She hurried after Tucker. Fifteen minutes ago, she'd wanted to avoid him. Now, the idea of leaving was absurd.

There were seasons in life. Maybe this was their season of friendship, and maybe it wouldn't hurt to let him in for a short time, just because they both seemed to need someone.

Maybe she was fooling herself. For the moment, it didn't matter. Shay mattered, and Tucker mattered. She hurried down the path, catching up with Tucker as he ate up the ground with long-legged strides.

"It's too cold out," he started.

She threw him what she hoped was a warning look. "I'm not fragile, and I'm wearing a jacket. I want to help Shay, and you."

He slowed his steps, making it easier for her to keep up. "I'm glad you're here."

She smiled up at him. "I'm more company than real help."

"I'll take it," he said as he headed in the direction of the creek. "Why does my sister seem bent on ripping the heart out of her own daughter?"

"I really wish I could tell you," Clara answered, still hurrying to keep up with him. The quick pace caused her abdomen to spasm painfully. She hesitated, taking a deep breath until the pain edged away.

Tucker had noticed, and he slowed down for her to catch up.

"I know you don't want to be questioned, but I do

worry about you." His gaze drifted to where her hand rested.

"I'm fine, just a stitch in my side from trying to keep up with you."

His expression changed. "Are you sure? You don't have to come with me. As much as I want you to…"

She cut him off. "I'm really okay. Let's find Shay. And tell me about this sister of yours, because I'm starting to dislike her."

"You and me both," he said. "My sister has always been one of the most decent people that I know. She's intelligent and kind. I've got no clue why she's doing this to her own kid."

"Maybe she's so lost in her own life she doesn't realize what she's doing to Shay?" She pointed to a bench near the creek, where his niece sat, hunched over against the cold.

"What do I say to her?"

"Ask her what happened. Let her talk. Tell her these feelings are temporary. When I came to Nan, I was hurting and angry, and Nan told me that I wouldn't always feel that way. She promised me that life had ups and downs and we're guaranteed both, but the bad times don't last." She drew in a breath, realizing that those words were still true.

"These should have been the best years for her," Tucker said. "Instead, she's having to deal with the damage her parents have done."

"But she has you," Clara reassured him as she squeezed his hand. "She wants her mom. She wants to know her parents haven't forgotten her, but she also knows that you love her and you're here for her."

"I wish I was enough," he said.

"You're her safety net, even though she might not recognize that right now. Go talk to her, Tucker."

"Thank you," he said so gently that it felt like an embrace.

Her heart pinged, and without thinking, she took a physical step back from him, from the dangerous wave of emotions that hit her all at once. She would blame it on the little person growing inside her, causing all of the hormonal and emotional turmoil.

But she knew better.

He had to walk away. The distance she'd put between them had been obvious. Tucker wasn't much of a ladies' man, but he knew when someone was trying to keep her walls up. That was probably the type of woman he knew best.

He tried not to take it personally. With Clara, he knew it was less personal and more about her current situation. He should thank her for reminding him why he needed to not get too involved.

Besides, Shay needed all of his attention right now. The messed-up relationship between her parents had them in this situation. The last thing she needed was more adult drama.

Tucker hesitated, but then he headed for his niece. She saw him and wiped tears from her face before she turned away.

"Shay?"

"I don't want to talk," Shay told him. "I just… I want to go home. I want to go to my house with my cat. I don't have a cat anymore."

"I'm sorry," he told her as he sat down on the bench beside her. "Why do you think you don't have a cat?"

"My mom told me. When she called, she told me that she wouldn't be here for Christmas, and she said she had to get rid of Hank because no one was there to take care of him."

Tucker wanted to hit something. He wanted to tell his sister what a selfish person she was. He wanted to fix all of this for his niece.

He sat there for a moment, trying to gather his thoughts, trying to figure out a way forward for Shay, something that would bring healing to her battered heart.

"I heard Tilly has some kittens," he offered, knowing it wouldn't fix anything.

She gave him a sideways look. "I do like kittens."

"We can call your mom and figure this whole thing out," he offered.

"I don't want to talk to her for a while," Shay informed him. "She won't even notice."

"She'll notice," he assured his niece. After the conversation he planned to have with his sister, she would take notice.

He didn't know yet what he would tell her, but he knew one thing—he wouldn't allow her to keep hurting Shay. He would do whatever he had to in order to keep his niece safe and happy.

"I started to climb a tree," Shay said quietly, almost smiling. "I heard a noise, and it scared me. I'm a city girl, you know."

He laughed at her. "I think what you heard was a rabbit hopping around in dry leaves."

"Oh. Well, it sounded bigger."

"Sasquatch?" he teased.

Shay laughed.

"We'll fix this, Shay. I promise. I don't know how, but we will figure it out." He took her hand and together they stood.

As they walked back to where Clara waited for them, she moved away from the tree she'd leaned against. Shay pulled free from him and ran to the waiting arms of the woman who had become far more than a housekeeper.

He had to keep reminding himself she was only temporary. Just one more person Shay would miss. He would miss her, too.

"I'm sorry for worrying everyone," Shay said as she hugged Clara. "I needed to be alone for a few minutes."

"We understand," Clara said consolingly. "But now let's get back to the church, because my feet are frozen and I think it's about to start raining."

Tucker couldn't agree more. As they walked, he caught the grimace of pain on Clara's face, the slight hesitation in her step. Cold feet were the least of their concerns.

"Are you going to make it?" he asked as he moved to her side.

"I'm fine. I chose to come with you."

"But you're not okay," he said.

"Of course I am."

He reached for her hand, ignoring the very knowing look that Shay gave him. She grinned, then she ran ahead to where Quinn waited with Avery and Grayson.

Avery gave the girl a quick look, holding her face in her hands, then dropped a kiss on Shay's forehead. After that, she focused on Clara, whose steps now lagged, and the tightness around her mouth gave evidence that she clearly wasn't okay. Tucker was tempted to pick her up and carry her back to the church, where it would be warm and she could rest.

"Are you all right, Clara?" Avery asked.

"I'm cold, and I'd like some hot tea," Clara said, dismissing her foster sister's concern. "Let's go home and make cookies."

As if nothing was wrong.

"No," Tucker said. "You're not okay and I think you need more than drinking hot tea and baking cookies."

"Excuse me?" she said.

"You heard me," he said, standing his ground.

"I don't think this is any of your business."

"Maybe not, but I'm—" He decided to stop there because she was giving him a death glare.

"We need to take Nan home," Clara said. "It's cold, and she won't be happy if we keep her from putting together her meals for senior housing."

Tucker made quick eye contact with Avery and took the obvious hint in her expression. He walked away, leaving the two sisters to have a discussion that didn't need to include him.

He'd done his part. She needed Avery right now, not him. She needed her family and not her interfering, temporary employer.

But oh, how he wanted to be the one to help her! Even if she didn't want his help.

Chapter Eleven

"I want you to let me examine you," Avery said after Tucker had walked away.

Clara wished she had gone with him. "I'm fine."

"Clara, you're pregnant, and you're obviously having some type of pain. Please, let me make sure everything is okay. We can drive over to the clinic, and I can do an ultrasound."

Ultrasound. That was the last thing Clara wanted to see. Not because she didn't care about the baby's health, but because seeing that little being on a screen would make it real, too real.

"It won't hurt, I promise," Avery insisted. "And then we can go back to Nan's and help with the senior meals."

Clara didn't plan to turn around and seek Tucker, but when she did her gaze connected with his. Whatever he saw in her expression had him moving back to her side.

"Clara?" he asked, his voice low and rumbling, making her feel safer, less afraid.

"We're going to my office," Avery told him. But he knew, so it wasn't as if there was a secret to keep.

Tucker ignored Avery and looked directly at Clara,

his hazel eyes warm and concerned. "Do you want me to go with you?"

She did, but she didn't. She'd let him cross every imaginary boundary she'd set for herself. No one had ever managed to get this deep into her life, no one except Nan and Avery.

She thought about the night of the attack, when the police officer had asked if he could call someone for her. Later, at the hospital, the doctor had asked the same thing. Each time she'd told them no, there was no one to call.

Now, with Avery standing at her side and Tucker willing to be with her, she realized she'd been wrong to say no. She should have called Nan. She should have called Avery.

She couldn't say no to Tucker. "Would you go with us?"

The words weren't easy for a person who had always striven to be independent and to keep people out of her bubble.

"Shay can ride to the house with Grayson and Quinn," Avery offered. "Tucker, do you want to drive us to the clinic?"

"I'd be happy to."

Fifteen minutes later they drove through the neighboring town of Riverview and pulled up to the pregnancy clinic where Avery had worked for the past six months. She unlocked the door for them and flipped on lights as they walked through the building. Clara shivered, not from the cold.

Tucker's arm went around her, and he pulled her close briefly. "I'll wait in here for you."

He indicated the small waiting room, which had a

few chairs and a table covered in magazines. Clara nodded and followed Avery down the hall.

"We have a brand-new 3D ultrasound," Avery said proudly as they entered an exam room. "I can print pictures for you."

Clara shook her head. "I don't want to see the baby."

Avery looked startled, her eyes widening. "Why don't you want to see the baby? Clara, please talk to me."

Clara closed her eyes briefly. She had to face this. She had to open up to her family. It wasn't easy to shed a lifetime of habits. She'd spent her childhood guarding her secrets, knowing it was safer to keep to herself.

But now she was an adult. Not a scared child.

"I love you, Clara. You're my sister," Avery said, ever the patient one.

"I know." Clara moved to the examining table and hopped on. "Let's get this done."

"You're not going to talk?" Avery prodded.

Clara looked at the ceiling, then she sighed, needing the release. "I was attacked in the parking garage at work."

"Oh, Clara! Why didn't you tell us?"

Clara gave her a beseeching look. "Because I'm stubborn, and I don't always realize how much I need you all."

Tears streaked down her cheeks, and Avery's also. Then she grabbed Clara close, hugging her. "You are stubborn. I'm so sorry that you went through this alone."

"I'm not alone now."

"No, you're not." Avery dried her eyes. "Let's take a look at you and see what's going on. I'm guessing you haven't been to an obstetrician."

"No, I haven't. Avery, I'm going to give the baby up for adoption."

Avery nodded, ever the pragmatist. "I'm not going to judge you for that. None of us knows what we would do in this situation. You have to do what is best for you."

"Thank you." Clara stretched out on the table, shaking from nerves as Avery prepared to do the ultrasound.

"Relax."

"Easy for you to say."

Avery gave her a steady look. "And as long as I've got you here, what's the deal between you and Tucker?"

"He's my boss."

Avery quirked a brow. "Really, because I've never hugged my boss."

"My boss is a friend, and he knows I won't be here for long. It's a temporary job."

Avery moved the ultrasound wand over her sister's abdomen. "Right, of course."

Clara started to glance at the screen, but then she turned her head away, not wanting to see the image. Her baby. She tamped down all her regrets and sorrow.

"Do you want to see?" Avery asked.

"Is the baby okay?" Clara asked.

"Definitely. Very healthy. I think the pains you're experiencing are just normal growing pains. Things stretching and growing can sometimes cause cramping."

Clara nodded, her eyes squeezed shut. "Can you tell if it is a boy or a girl?"

"I can." Avery's voice was soft, wondering. The voice of a woman who loved her job and the mystery of childbirth.

"I don't want to know."

"I'll print a picture and put it in an envelope for you. When you're ready, you can look."

"Thank you."

"You're welcome," Avery said as she moved away. "Clara, I'm glad you told me. I'm also glad you agreed to be examined. Please take care of yourself."

"I will. I promise." Clara slid off the table.

"I'm going to clean up. Go talk to Tucker. Tell him the baby is healthy and that you're fine."

The last thing Tucker needed, with everything going on in his life, was a woman who pictured her anxiety as an elephant and who would soon leave town.

She told him that the baby was healthy and so was she. Tucker took her by the hand and led her outside, to his truck. He helped her inside, leaning in to kiss her cheek.

When Avery joined them, the truck was blanketed in silence.

"I'm hungry," Avery said as they drove to Nan's.

"Same," Tucker agreed.

Clara let the two of them carry the conversation while she stared at the manila envelope Avery had dropped in her lap.

When they arrived at the farm, Nan was at the stove, heating the soup she'd made the previous evening. Grayson was slicing the homemade bread.

Spending Sunday at Nan's was a time-honored tradition for all girls who had spent time in this home. In Clara's case, that first Sunday lunch had been life-changing. It was the day she realized she no longer had to fight for a sandwich or hide food in her bedroom. At Nan's there would always be plenty of warm meals and time together. Those lunches had symbolized more than food: they had been about a safe place and family.

Once again, Clara needed this place, the meal, the warmth and the family. She needed Nan's hugs. The thought of those hugs, of the woman who gave them freely, and then watching her succumb to dementia were especially difficult to accept today.

"You know you're going to be okay, don't you?" Nan told Clara as she moved to her foster mother's side. "I know it doesn't feel that way, but it's the truth."

"I know," Clara agreed. She believed it today more than she had the past few months, since that night, the first of August, when she thought she would never be okay ever again.

She'd gone to church. She'd gone to counseling. She'd come home. She was healing. Little by little.

"We're all going to be okay," Nan said, a little too brightly. "Would you men go feed for me? This cold rain is hard on an old lady's bones."

Grayson and Tucker grabbed their jackets and hats off the hooks by the door and left the women alone. Avery laughed a little.

"So that's how you get them out from under your feet," she said.

"Of course it is," Nan said. "They feel sorry for me, so they're willing to do whatever I ask."

Avery caught Clara's attention. The two of them shared a somber smile, knowing they were going to be facing one of the most difficult times in their lives. Losing Nan. And Nan would tell them they were going to be just fine. It would just take a while to believe that they would be okay.

Nan reached for the paper towels, tore off a few

sheets and handed them out. "Let's dry our eyes and focus on what is good. We are more than conquerors through Jesus who gives us strength. And since we don't know if this rain will stop, I have a plan for today."

"What's your plan?" Avery asked as she put the buttered bread on a plate.

"Several things," Nan said with a mischievous twinkle in her eyes. "After lunch, we'll bake our cookies. I made a pot full of soup, and I already divided it in containers to deliver to our friends at the seniors' apartments."

"Okay, cookies first," Clara said. "And then?"

"I know you girls don't want to hear this, but I want to start my memory book. I want to go through old photos and place the pictures in a book with stories about each of you and the things we've done together. Not just the good things. I want the hard memories, too."

"Nan," Clara started, her eyes welling up with tears for the third, maybe fourth time in the past hour.

"Now, don't start that again. I have memories still to be made with you all." She smiled first at Avery and Clara before turning to the two younger girls who had returned to the kitchen. "I have grandchildren to spoil and life to live, and I plan on living it to the fullest. I'm even thinking about going on a cruise."

"I want to go!" Quinn hurried forward and wrapped her arms around Nan.

Clara was still stuck on the subject of Nan's grandchildren. The child she carried, had the circumstances been different, would have been a grandchild to Nan. She found it difficult to breathe.

The door opened, and the men entered. Grayson came first, wiping his feet on the rug and then pulling off his jacket and hat. Tucker followed, going through the same routine after first handing over an old coffee container filled with eggs that had been gathered from the hen house. He kicked off his boots and set them next to the door and then hung up his rain-soaked cowboy hat. He ran a hand through his short hair, making the curls spring back to life. Avery shot Clara a knowing look.

"We should eat," Clara said, ignoring her foster sister.

"That's a good idea," Nan said. "I think we have everything on the table. Grayson or Tucker, would one of you pray, please."

Grayson nodded to Tucker. Clara bowed her head and closed her eyes tight, adding her own prayer to the blessing on their food. *God, give me strength*, she prayed silently.

They sat around the big table with its bench seats on the sides and chairs on each end. Nan sat at the head of the table as she'd done for so many meals during Clara's teen years. Some days up to a half dozen girls would have been seated here. Grayson had taken a spot on the bench, next to his wife and daughter. Tucker sat at the end opposite Nan, and Shay was next to Clara. They weren't all family, but when it came to meals at Nan's, everyone was connected.

Clara was nearly finished eating when her phone buzzed with a notification. She glanced and saw that it was an email.

"Is everything okay?" Avery asked.

"Just an email." Clara glanced at her notifications. Two emails. She opened the app.

One email was from her employer, offering her a position in Mexico. Based in a coastal town on a beautiful tourist-destination island. She would have an apartment on the property and a car at her disposal. Jobs like this rarely came open, and they were offering it to her.

It would mean leaving Pleasant, leaving Nan, Avery and her family. Leaving Tucker and Shay. The thought took her by surprise. Tucker shouldn't be part of her regrets, the people she would miss. From the beginning she'd known that this position was short-term. Their relationship was a working relationship only.

The second message was from the adoption agency, asking her to finish the paperwork so they could match her unborn baby with a family.

Conversation at the table continued. Nan was discussing a boat she'd sold to some corporate bigwig from Nashville. Shay and Quinn were discussing the Christmas caroling scheduled for that evening, if the rain stopped.

Clara put her phone on the bench next to her, planning to rejoin the conversation. Across the table, Tucker watched her, questions in his hazel eyes. She didn't have answers.

The one thing she knew for certain was that she wouldn't be in Pleasant long enough to fall in love with him, and that was probably a very good thing.

Even if it felt a little too late.

The table was being cleared when Tucker's phone rang. He glanced at the caller ID and groaned. His sister was the last person he wanted to deal with at the moment. Fortunately Shay didn't seem to notice.

Clara, of course, saw and she gave him a questioning look. He left the room and paced through the house, finding a small room at the end of the downstairs hall that most likely belonged to Nan. There were photos of her girls, paintings of the river and worn leather furniture. He stalked to the window and watched as cold rain fell.

The room would hopefully give him privacy for whatever conversation would ensure. With his sister, he no longer knew from one day to the next what she'd say or do.

"Jana," he practically growled as he answered.

She didn't answer and he wondered if she'd hung up. After several seconds she responded.

"How's Shay?" she asked.

"You mean your daughter?" he asked.

"You know who I mean," Jana said. "I thought I'd see what you're planning for Christmas."

"What I'm planning for Christmas, for your daughter." He managed to keep his tone level. "You're someone I no longer recognize. The Jana I grew up with, the woman who had a daughter that she and her husband doted on, wouldn't ignore that child and act as if her feelings don't matter. Jana, you and Kyle had a marriage that I envied. You have a daughter who is the best of both of you. She needs the two of you to put her first."

He listened to his sister make excuses about their jobs and trying to figure things out. Most of what he heard sounded as if his sister was only thinking of herself.

"Get your act together, and figure out your life. And until then, don't call Shay. I won't let you keep hurting her. If I have to... I don't know, maybe I'll file for custody." He listened as she began to tell him why he couldn't do that to her. Then he said, "Everything out of your mouth is about you, Jana. It's about your feelings and how this will affect you. I'm going to find a way to stop you from hurting her."

She hung up on him. He moved away from the window and the winter cold that seemed to permeate the glass, even though the room was warm. Soon he realized he wasn't alone. Clara stood in the doorway.

"How'd it go?" she asked.

"I tried to get my sister to admit her daughter should come first," he told her. "I'm not sure if she heard a word I said."

"I'm praying for Shay and her parents," Clara told him. "I'm sure they care. Even good people sometimes lose their way."

"I feel like I no longer know my sister," he admitted. "But you're right, people make mistakes. Hopefully they realize that before it's too late."

Clara said nothing.

"Are *you* okay?" he asked.

She smiled at him. "I'm good. It's just a lot, being here with Nan, in this house. So much is going on and…" She shrugged, and he thought she probably wouldn't tell him everything. "But I didn't come in here to talk about me. I wanted to see if you needed anything."

"A sister who understands what she's doing to her daughter would be nice."

"I hope you have her back, soon."

"Me, too," he said, moving toward her. Drawn to her. "What's everyone else doing?"

"Shay and Quinn are making cookies." She grinned. "I helped."

He smiled at that. "How'd that go?"

Her chocolate-brown eyes twinkled. "I mixed the dry ingredients. I might have put in one cup of salt and a half a teaspoon of sugar. Apparently that was wrong, and they were all appalled."

"It could happen to anyone," he said gently as he reached for her hand. "I'm sure it's not that bad."

She smiled up at him. "That's sweet of you to say. Nan would disagree. She had to toss it and start over. Fortunately, she also made a batch of cookies last night."

She touched her belly, and he couldn't help but be worried about her.

"Are you sure you're okay?" he asked.

"I am." She let go of his hand and headed for the door. "We should join the others. The girls sent Grayson to the basement for the Christmas decorations. Tucker?" she said.

"Yes?" He narrowed the distance between them.

"I'm going to miss you," she said. "When I go, I'll miss you and Shay."

"I'll miss you, too." He leaned until his face hovered above hers. Her warm brown eyes sought something from him.

"Clara," he whispered as he touched his lips to hers.

"Uncle Tucker, are you going to try the cookies we made?" Shay's voice from down the hall split them quickly apart.

He released Clara so quickly she almost lost her balance, and he had to steady her.

Rather than look upset, she looked amused.

"Whoops," she said as they stood there staring into each other's eyes. He was so taken by surprise that he wasn't quite sure what to do or say.

Shay appeared in the doorway behind Clara. "We have the first batch finished."

"We're coming," Tucker told her.

Shay looked from Clara to Tucker and rolled her eyes.

"For real?" she asked.

"For real." He ushered his niece back down the hall but glanced back, just in time to catch Clara with two fingers pressed to her lips and a faintly amused look on her face.

They met Grayson coming out of the basement.

"Some help would be nice, man," Grayson huffed as he handed a tub over to Tucker.

"Right, of course. Let me take this for you," Tucker said as he hefted the container. "What else can I get?"

"If you take those to the living room, I can get the last of the decorations," Grayson suggested.

"No problem." Tucker headed for the living room where, it appeared, Grayson had already unloaded the contents of nearly the entire basement. As he set the tub down with the rest of the decorations, he could hear Shay's laughter and then the excited voice of Quinn. Nan said something, then he heard Clara's laughter threading through the conversation.

He left the living room, drawn by the sound of conversation and laughter.

At the door to the kitchen, he paused. Shay and Quinn stood behind Nan, watching as she stirred something in a sauce pan. The smell of warm peanut butter and chocolate permeated the room. If he had to guess, he'd say that Nan was making fudge.

His gaze connected with Clara's. She leaned, hip against the counter, taking notes as Nan cooked. Her smile was sweet and shy. What a picture they made as they clustered around the old woman.

"Tucker, there are cookies," Nan said as she checked the candy thermometer. "Of course, it won't be long and we'll also have fudge."

"Your fudge is the best." He took a cookie and then he walked to the window.

He needed something to do. Something that would get his mind off…everything. He glanced out the window at gray skies and the rain that continued to pelt the windows.

"Do you think we'll get to go caroling tonight?" he asked no one in particular.

"I hope so," Shay told him. "I've never been caroling. Also, Nan has a lot of soup ready to deliver."

"I think it's supposed to end by late afternoon," Grayson informed them as he entered the room. "Until then, we have a tree to decorate."

Nan handed a spoon to Quinn, who took over stirring the fudge. "I think decorating the tree while we're all here is the perfect plan."

Grayson moved to his side, a cookie in each hand. Tucker wouldn't doubt if he didn't also have them in his pockets.

"You're worse than the kids."

Grayson grinned. "And I don't plan on changing. Let's get the tree put up for these girls to decorate."

"Good idea," Tucker agreed.

He didn't move, though. He enjoyed being in the kitchen with these people. The smells, the sounds, the way they talked and laughed as they cooked, it all felt like coming home.

He thought of his sister, hundreds of miles away,

missing out on these moments with her daughter. Maybe she didn't care. Whatever was going on with Kyle and Jana, he hoped they figured it out before it was too late.

"The tree?" Grayson reminded, drawing Tucker's attention.

"Yep, sounds like a plan." Tucker poured himself a cup of coffee and followed his friend from the room.

The living room was crowded with boxes and plastic tubs. Sugar was curled up on her dog bed, studying the mess as if she couldn't understand how her world had gone from peaceful to chaotic. The dog gave them a critical look as they started to unbox the tree.

"Where should we put the tree?" Tucker asked.

"I think she puts it in the corner, away from the window and the fireplace." Grayson grabbed the base and set it in the spot he'd mentioned. "Here?"

Tucker shrugged. "Looks good to me."

From the kitchen, Christmas music blared and five women's voices, young and old, sang along. A guy couldn't help but smile. Between the rain falling, the smell of cookies fresh from the oven and the impromptu concert of women singing "Joy to the World," it wasn't such a bad day.

The women joined them soon after the song was over. The tree was up, and Tucker and Grayson had unpacked the ornaments. Some of them appeared to be decades old. A few were new. It wasn't going to be one of those trees with color-coordinated decorations.

Nan peered into a box. "Look at this. I think Avery made this in art class." She held up a clear globe with a star inside. The glitter had fallen off.

"How did you get the star in there?" Quinn asked.

"The ornament came in two pieces. The star went

inside, and we glued it to keep it together." Avery took the ornament from Nan and held it up to the light. "I was so proud of this."

"It's beautiful," Grayson told her as he put his arms around her. His hands went to his wife's belly, a fleeting touch that they probably hadn't meant to share.

Tucker glanced at Clara and saw the flash of pain in her eyes. She'd witnessed the gentleness between the couple and probably understood what that moment meant. Tucker's guess was that his friends were having a baby of their own but hadn't shared the news yet.

Nan continued to pull out ornaments, telling stories with each. Clara took pictures and, he guessed, a few videos on her phone.

In a second tub, Nan pulled out a smaller box. She handed it to Clara. "The nativity you bought me for Christmas. Your second year with me, I think. You should put that on the mantel."

Clara took the box, her eyes shiny with tears. She hugged Nan tight before walking away with the nativity set. As everyone else continued to decorate the tree, Clara unpacked the nativity and set it out on the mantel. She positioned each figure, pausing with Mary and the baby Jesus, holding them as if they were precious to her. Tucker forced his attention away from Clara and the nativity. She obviously needed a moment, and he needed to focus on Shay.

The two girls were stringing lights around the tree. He hoped Shay and Quinn would always be friends.

"Hey, dude, why don't you put this on the stair railing?" Grayson handed him a long section of green garland.

"I don't know if I'm artistic enough for wrapping garlands on stairs." Tucker set his coffee down and headed for the open staircase at the back of Nan's living room. "Look, the sun is coming out."

"Is it? I think you might be imagining things. Or maybe that is wishful thinking?" Avery teased.

She dropped the subject and glanced at Clara who was still lining up the nativity display.

Tucker followed that look and watched as Clara continued to decorate the fireplace, adding a few battery-operated candles, a few red ornaments and an angel.

Shay and Quinn were laughing as they strung aging gold tinsel on the tree. A few strings of it had come loose, and they were blowing them around in the air. The two girls started singing "Deck the Halls," and Avery and Grayson joined in. Nan's sweet soprano carried the chorus. It seemed like the perfect Sunday, except for the look on Clara's face.

He turned away because the sweetness of her expression combined with her aura of sadness somehow burrowed its way into his heart, making him want to fix whatever had hurt her. And hurt whoever had taken her joy.

Chapter Twelve

Clara had a secret she'd never told anyone: Christmas broke her heart. Every year she started on a firm foothold, intending to love the holiday, the lights, the gift giving and the food. Somewhere along the way, memories would resurface and steal her joy. She'd had long talks with herself about those memories. She didn't have to let them in. She could push them aside and make new memories. She could focus on only the good.

The problem with being human was that it didn't always work out that way. This year appeared to be no exception. Except this year she had Clyde the Elephant to deal with a tiny human being counting on her to make the right choices for their future. Plus, she had all of the lovely people surrounding her and a job offer in Mexico.

She couldn't ignore the tiny human because it constantly made its presence known with nausea, an ever-expanding belly and the cramps she'd been experiencing for the past two weeks.

With the tree decorated and dusk stealing the day's brief flirtation with sunlight and blue skies, the family had decided that caroling was back on the agenda.

Nan had sent the men to get boxes for the food and to warm up the vehicles. The girls were quickly donning their jackets, boots and gloves.

Clara slipped her feet into her boots and wrapped a scarf around her neck. "Nan, let me carry that box."

She took a box from her foster mother.

"Be careful out there. We don't want you to fall." Nan patted her cheek. "You're going to be fine, sweetie."

"Thank you, Nan." Clara carried the box out the back door but only made it to the porch steps before Tucker was there.

"I'll take that," he said in his I'm-the-man voice.

"I can carry a box," she argued.

"I know you can," he argued back. "But I'd like to do this for you."

"I'm pregnant, not weak."

"My dad taught me to open doors, carry the heavy boxes and never swear in front of a lady," he explained.

She couldn't help but smile. "Your father is an exceptional gentleman."

She relinquished the box to him and hurried back inside for her purse. Nan was coming out of the house with Shay and Quinn. She handed Clara's purse to her.

"Let's get this show on the road," Nan said. "Who is riding where?"

"We're riding with my mom and dad," Quinn shouted as she grabbed Shay by the hand and dragged her to Grayson's truck.

"That was easy," Grayson said. "Nan, where do you want to ride? We put most of the food in Tucker's back seat. Before I forget, Pastor Wilson said they'll meet us at the senior housing. They have a few kids to pick up in the church van."

"If the food is in Tucker's truck, I'll ride with you, Grayson. Clara, do you mind going along with Tucker?"

As if she had a choice. But she didn't voice that sentiment. She smiled at Tucker. "Looks like you're stuck with me. Are you going to open that door for me?"

He laughed. "My dad would be disappointed if I didn't."

As she stood next to him, she felt a mixture of so many things. Being overwhelmed by his presence seemed to be at the forefront; attraction and fear were a close second. She broke the connection by looking away as he moved to the passenger side of his truck to open the door.

Maybe if she got in and just spent the five-minute drive looking out the window at passing scenery that was being enveloped by the early winter sunset, maybe then she would be able to put her emotions in order. The darkness was quickly eating away at the tiny glimmer of blue skies they'd enjoyed.

In no time they were pulling into the parking lot of the apartment complex of single-story duplexes. They appeared to be the first ones there.

"Where's Grayson?" Clara asked as they got out of the truck.

Tucker shrugged those massive shoulders of his. "I'm not sure. He was right behind me but turned into town. Maybe to pick someone up? But then, he wouldn't have room in his truck for any more people." He studied her face for a moment. "Back at the house, were you upset about something?"

"I'm fine," she said with a careful smile. Isn't that what people did? They smiled, they laughed, they pretended to be okay because anything else made others uncomfortable?

"Nah," he said. "I'm not buying it. You can fool other people with those smiles and your laughter, but I saw the look on your face when you were setting up the nativity."

"So now you think you know me."

He didn't back down. "Yep."

"You're a nuisance, you know that?" She opened the back door of the truck to pull out one of the packaged meals.

"The nativity?" he said softly, as he took the food from her.

"I bought it for Nan because I had always wanted one as a child. To me, it was a symbol of a happy family. I think because at my friends' homes, I'd come to connect their faith, the nativity, all that they had as a family, to happiness."

"And you weren't happy."

"When I was ten, my fifth-grade teacher gave me a nativity set. We'd talked about Christmas and what I'd love to have more than anything else, and that's what I'd asked for. When I took it home, my dad told me not to accept charity and threw it in the trash pile and burned it."

"Wow," he said.

"Right?" She managed to smile and meet his concerned and angry gaze. She couldn't allow herself to put too much into that look of his. "Don't waste time being upset for me. It was a long time ago. Today the nativity is about something more. It's about a birth. About a young girl who took on something that changed not only her life but the lives of everyone around her. The baby in a manger is a symbol of hope and faith. For Mary and Joseph that manger was life-altering. A young girl and a carpenter, they would have settled in their small village and lived inconsequential lives. Do you think they knew just how much His birth would change them? She was just a young girl, and she told God, 'Use me.' Joseph had to accept the task that God had for him. He had to make a conscious decision to trust God, to trust his wife and to take on a burden that wasn't his. I'm a grown woman, and I can only think *Why me?*"

"Your situation is drastically different," he reminded her without even a hint of a smile, and she was thinking she should laugh at herself for being so dramatic. He gave her a questioning look. "No one is going to judge you for deciding what you think is right for you and your baby."

"I know." She glanced down, at her hands splayed across her belly. She hadn't even realized she was doing it. "I got an email from the adoption agency. They need all of my personal information, and they want me to tell them what I know about my attacker. Because, of course, anyone who is interested in adopting this child is going to want to know those details."

"I'm sorry," he said.

"Me, too," she said. "I can't say that I never dreamed about getting married and having children. I could picture myself with a husband, the two of us together, maybe singing to our unborn child. Instead, I'm thinking about choosing the couple who will eventually take my baby. Should I still talk to it and comfort it?"

She quieted, her hand still on her belly. A tear trickled down her cheek.

"Give me your hand," she told him.

She waited for him to set the food in the back seat, then she took the large, strong hand he held out to her and placed it on her belly. She put her hand over it and guided him to a spot near her belly button.

"What is it?" he asked, watching her face as she moved his hand.

"The baby moved." She said it with wonder because she hadn't expected to feel such emotion during this moment. "Wait."

It happened again. The tiny being inside her jumped, and her belly moved, more a twitch than anything else.

"I felt it," he said, a voice of wonder that matched what she felt.

She flicked away a second tear. "Pregnancy hormones are the worst. It isn't something to cry over."

"I think it's pretty tear worthy," he told her.

She saw that he'd started crying as well.

"Kiss me," she whispered.

He touched his lips to hers. For a moment, she forgot that they were in a public place and sighed, bringing a hand up to the nape of his neck.

He kissed her sweetly and then pulled back slightly, kissing her temple, then just holding her. After he moved away from her, she couldn't look into his eyes. What if he regretted the kiss? She couldn't look, not when she was battling herself, trying to figure out what it was she truly felt for him.

Suddenly Grayson's truck and then the white church van pulled in to the parking lot and took the spaces near Tucker's truck. "Looks like the cavalry has arrived."

"I'm not sure I wanted reinforcements," he teased her.

Clara took those words and put them away for future contemplation. She didn't want to overthink what was happening between them. She just wanted a little joy in her life right now.

But those pregnancy hormones had different ideas.

A few minutes later, he and Clara were surrounded by a group of laughing, chatting teenagers. Pastor Wilson and his wife, along with another youth minister, tried to herd the kids and keep them focused as they unloaded the vehicles, grabbing the boxes of food prepared by Nan and other members of the church.

They were fighting a losing battle trying to contain those kids, but all in good fun.

As the group finished handing out food to the first apartment they moved on to the second. They began to sing another carol, their voices soft in the quiet of early evening as dusk began to spread from the west. Tucker found himself near the rear of the group and next to Clara.

When she looked up at him, she seemed to be biting her cheek and trying to control herself.

"What?" he asked, but he couldn't help the way his lips tugged upward.

"You look like you'd rather be dipped in honey and rolled in an anthill than spend the next hour with this group."

"And that's amusing to you?" he said, chuckling.

"A little, yes."

The door to an apartment opened. He realized that most of the apartment doors had now opened and residents had stepped out to stand on their porches to watch the church carolers move through the complex.

"I'm actually having a very good time," Tucker said, remaining at Clara's side.

The group reached the next apartment, a petite lady with long gray hair, enveloped in a floor-length flannel robe, stood in the doorway. She wore a grin that widened as the church kids began to sing "Away in a Manger."

Tucker pulled out his phone and began to video the moment. Shay stood in the crowd, singing brightly with her arms around Quinn and another girl. The three harmonized as they started the first verse of "Silent Night."

They sang only one verse of each song because no one wanted to make the seniors stand in the cold longer than necessary. Nan stepped out of the crowd and handed the woman a box.

"Hadley, we want to wish you a Merry Christmas. If you need anything, don't hesitate to call."

"Thank you all so much, and come back soon. I'll make the cookies next time." Hadley waved and then stepped back inside, closing the door to the night and the cold.

The next apartment belonged to Tom Jackson. He'd always been a bit of a curmudgeon around town. Tucker remembered him from years ago, hollering at kids for riding their bikes past his house, complaining about the ladies in town planting too many flowers that drew bees, which he was allergic to.

"Do we have to go here?" a boy of about fifteen asked.

"Yes, we do," said Pastor Wilson. "Riley, why wouldn't we go to Mr. Jackson's?"

"Last year he chased my dog with his cane. Scooter

was on a leash at the park, but Mr. Jackson said he knew for a fact that dogs were killing off the songbirds."

"Let's give Tom a chance. It's Christmas, after all." Pastor Wilson handed the boy a box with the soup, rolls and cookies. "Your turn, Riley."

Tucker felt for the kid. Tom was a legend in this town. And not in a good way.

Riley took up the challenge. He stood a little straighter, knocked on the door and waited. Tom came to the door in all his glory. He wore a dour expression as easily as he wore his big overalls and rubber boots. His thinning gray hair was brushed back from his face, and he hadn't shaved in a few days. Tom might still be a bully, but he was probably in his eighties and not quite as intimidating as he'd once been.

"What do you want?" Tom asked the boy in front of him.

"We wanted to wish you a Merry Christmas, Mr. Jackson." Riley handed him the box of food as the students started singing "Silent Night."

Tom started to open his mouth as if he might run them off. As the group continued to sing, Tom visibly softened. He studied the group and nodded as they sang. Then, wonder of wonders, he began to sing along as they moved on to "Joy to the World."

"That was real nice," Tom said as the song ended. He cleared his throat and looked out at the kids gathered in front of his door. "I hope you all have a real good Christmas. Maybe I'll come over to that church for your Christmas service."

Pastor Wilson stepped forward to shake Tom's hand. "Tom, we'd like that."

"Now, don't go gettin' no ideas," he said, returning

to his typical self. "I ain't never been one for religion, and I'm not giving you no money."

"That's okay, Tom. We're not much for religion, either. But we're okay with finding faith." Pastor Wilson settled a hand on the old man's shoulder. "You call us if you need anything at all, you hear?"

"Thank you, Pastor. And Nan, I sure hope this is your beef soup."

Nan stepped forward and hugged him. "It's your lucky day, Tom Jackson. You behave yourself."

As they moved on to the next apartment, Tucker felt a hand slip into his. Clara looked up at him. She'd pulled on a white knit cap and it framed her face. She was shorter than most of the teens, not even reaching his shoulder. He felt a sudden and overwhelming need to keep her close, to keep her safe.

With her hand in his, it was hard to convince himself that he didn't feel anything for her. Those feelings took him by surprise, because they were unlike anything he'd ever experienced.

He knew that she wasn't looking for a relationship. She was looking for a new beginning somewhere far from their little river town.

But he wasn't a man who gave up easily. He knew, deep down, that Clara was worth fighting for.

Chapter Thirteen

Wednesday morning, Clara couldn't seem to get anything right. She'd burned the toast, and the eggs had stuck to the bottom of the frying pan. She put precooked bacon on a plate and stuck it in the microwave to crisp. Surely, she could do that right.

"The coffee!" Tucker yelled as he came running in to the kitchen.

Clara spun around, nearly losing her balance as a wave of dizziness hit. She grabbed the counter to steady herself, then she burst into tears when she saw the coffee pouring down the counter and the coffeepot in the sink.

Tucker slid into the kitchen, grabbed the pot and stuck it under the spout to catch the brew that was dripping out. Clara grabbed paper towels and got down on her knees to wipe up the mess. As she worked, tears kept falling. She wiped at them with her sleeve and grabbed another roll of paper towels.

"I'm so sorry," she told Tucker. "I'm not sure what's wrong with me."

"It's okay," he said. He squatted next to her, taking

the paper towels from her hands. He sprayed the floor and counter with cleaner and finished wiping up the mess as she sat next to him, her back against the cabinet door.

The tears had dried, and she giggled. "I'm an absolute mess of a housekeeper. It's a good thing I have other skills."

"You're pretty decent at laundry," he said, jollying her. "And Tilly said you're an expert at ordering takeout."

"Everyone has to have a skill. At least I know mine." She took another clean paper towel from him and wiped her face. "I really am sorry."

"Stop apologizing. It could happen to anyone." He stood, and then he reached for her, drawing her to her feet. "I'll make a deal with you. I'll take Shay to school early enough that she can get breakfast there, and then I'll come back and take you to Tilly's."

"You understand I work for you, right?" In the past two weeks they had definitely crossed some boundaries. Maybe she needed to draw those lines again, because neither of them wanted to be hurt.

"I mean, I'm not very good at my job, but I do work for you."

"I know that." He gave her one of those dimpled grins that made her forget everything. "But we have to eat."

"We have burnt toast and eggs and a half pot of coffee."

"Sounds delicious," Shay said as she entered the kitchen, her backpack over her shoulder.

"No big plans for turning our lives upside down today?" Clara asked.

Shay shot her a look as she poured a bowl of cereal. "I heard the comment about school breakfast. I'll have cold cereal. And no big plans. I mean, I do have a list of possible scenarios that might make any adult cringe, but I'm determined to be good. Besides that, I like school now. They're giving me work and that makes it more interesting."

Clara gave the girl a hug. "That's good, because I don't enjoy cold walks in the woods. Not in December."

"Or even in June," Tucker chimed in. "And since you lost your phone privileges for a week, try to remember that there are consequences for your actions, okay?"

"Right, consequences." Shay slid her bowl across the counter and hopped on a stool to eat.

Tucker watched his niece for a moment, then he went for a cup of coffee. "I have a new bull being delivered today. But I might not be here to receive it. I have a meeting at church later this afternoon."

"Do you want me to unload the bull?" Clara asked, her eyes wide.

He laughed out loud. "No, I don't. I just wanted you to be aware that someone might be backing a trailer down to the barn and unloading a bull."

"As long as they can unload him themselves. I'm Nan's least farmhand kind of kid."

"Have you ever ridden a horse?" Shay asked.

"A few times, but not well."

"I like to ride. Uncle Tucker bought me a horse. Her name is Daisy. Maybe he'll teach you to ride?"

"Maybe someday," Clara said as she scraped the burnt eggs in the trash. "Oh, I forgot the bacon."

She pulled the bacon out of the microwave and tossed the paper towel she'd covered it with.

"Perfect," Shay said as she grabbed a slice. She finished her cereal, put the bowl in the dishwasher and picked up her backpack. "I'll take the bus this morning."

"Are you sure?" Tucker asked.

"I'm sure."

"I'll walk with you," Tucker told his niece. "I need to check the gate up by the road. It looked like someone messed with the lock."

After they left, Clara leaned hard against the counter and took a few deep breaths. From the window over the sink she could see Tucker and Shay as they walked together, and her heart hurt a little, thinking about the time when she would no longer be here, in Pleasant with them, with Nan and with her family.

It was all becoming so complicated. Her feelings for Tucker and for his niece. Her concern for Nan. And yet, she felt as if she had to get away. She needed to start over in a new job, in a new place. She knew she couldn't outrun the nightmares. She couldn't outrun the reality of what was going to happen in a matter of months.

Her phone dinged with an email notification. She read the short message from the adoption agency. It was instructions for an online video chat. They wanted to discuss the adoption with her.

She glanced out the window and saw Tucker walking with Dudley. They were heading toward the barn. Without really thinking it through, she put on her coat, slipped her feet into boots and walked out the back door. She crossed the lawn and walked down the grassy path to the barn.

Tucker was backing the tractor up to a bale of hay. He stopped and motioned for her to come forward.

"Climb up," he said. "Give me your hand."

"Is it safe?"

He grinned. He looked so cute sitting in the cab of his tractor, a ball cap pulled down over his light brown curls, her heart melted a little.

"It's safe," he said. "And it's warm in here."

She took his hand and climbed aboard the big, green tractor. He was right: it was warmer inside, and there was enough room for her to squeeze in next to him.

"I need to move a few bales. Are you up for the ride? It isn't the smoothest."

"I'm good."

He gave her a careful look as he backed up to hook a bale of hay. "Are you really?"

She shrugged. "I have a video chat with the adoption agency this morning."

"I see."

"I know it's the right thing to do." She watched out the window as they moved through the field with the hay.

In the distance she could see the herd of cattle. The cattle spotted the tractor and trotted over. Tucker stopped, glanced back at the bale, then started forward again.

Clara watched as the bale unrolled. The cattle moved in, grazing as the hay hit the ground. She couldn't explain it, but it was calming, to sit there in the tractor and watch this process. It was just the two of them, hundreds of acres and livestock.

"What time is your call?" he asked as they headed back to the round bales where he spiked another.

"In thirty minutes."

"I can be in there with you," he offered. "If you want."

The idea appealed to her, but then she thought about

how it would feel to have him watching her, judging her as she made the arrangements with strangers.

"I don't know," she answered truthfully.

"I understand."

He unrolled the next bale of hay. The cattle that had been grazing the strip of hay he'd left behind now moved to the new strip. She smiled as a calf ran, jumping and kicking, then hurried back to its mama.

"It's cute," she said. "I never was a farm kid, but I remember when I first came to Nan's, I used to like to walk through the field. There is something calming about walking through a pasture full of cattle."

"Yeah, I guess there is." He pulled through the gate, stopped the tractor and hopped down. "I have to close this. Do you want to drive the tractor?"

"I think that's a bad idea," she told him.

"Nah, I think you're a farm girl at heart."

He returned a moment later, climbing up to sit next to her. It was cozy in the cab of the tractor with him. Too cozy. An hour earlier she'd been telling herself to remember her boundaries, and here she was, practically sitting on his lap in the tractor.

"Grab the wheel," he told her.

When she did, he showed her how to accelerate.

The tractor jumped a little, and Tucker chuckled.

"Oops, sorry." She bit down on her bottom lip and focused as she headed for the barn. "Where do I park?"

"Equipment shed." He pointed to the three-sided building a short distance from the barn. A second tractor, a farm truck and a baler were also parked under the roof.

"I think I should let you take over now," she told him. "But I don't know how to stop this thing."

He took the wheel from her, and she scooted back over a bit, letting him take control. They were shoulder-to-shoulder, and he smelled of fresh air, hay and soap. With practiced ease, he backed the tractor into its space.

"There we go," he said.

"That's it?"

He flashed a quick grin. "Nah, I've got cattle across the road, too. But I fed them earlier this morning, long before you were awake. I'll help you down."

He climbed down from the tractor, reached up for her and eased her down the steps. They stood there for a moment as his farm dog chased something small around the tractor and then across the lawn.

"He thinks he's going to catch a mouse." Tucker shook his head. "He's never been able to catch one."

"You need a cat," she said.

"Yeah, Shay wants a kitten. I doubt it'll ever see the inside of a barn."

As they crossed to the house, she told him, "I have to do this alone," referring to the video call. "I thought about asking you to sit with me, but then I realized I can't keep doing this to you, dragging you into my life like this."

"I'm not being dragged," he told her.

"Maybe not, but we're definitely on some shaky ground here. I'm leaving soon, and you have Shay to think about. I was supposed to come here to work and help you, not to become another one of your problems."

"You aren't a problem, you're—"

She didn't let him finish that sentence. "I have to go inside. Leave me a list for today."

"No list," he told her. "And I'll pray for you."

"You're making this so difficult."

"Making what difficult?"

"I'm going to leave eventually, Tucker." She planted her hands on her hips, hoping to look determined and strong. "You make me want to stay…and I can't."

"Oh, believe me, I'm aware that you're going to leave."

She hurried away from him, afraid that if she stood there any longer, he would say something that might make her never want to leave.

The video chat started on time.

For thirty minutes she discussed the adoption, what she wanted, what she wanted for her baby. The agent assured her that if she signed with their organization, she would be very involved in the adoption process. She would meet the prospective parents if she wanted. She would get updates and photos of her child—again, if she wanted that connection. She wanted to say yes, she wanted all of this. She wanted to meet the parents. She wanted pictures. She tried to respond, but the words didn't come, only tears.

She'd never felt so broken, so alone in her life. Sitting there in Tucker Church's living room, she felt adrift. And as if to remind her what had started this process, the baby moved again, just a fleeting movement, not much more than butterfly wings inside her.

"Miss Fisher, are you okay?" Miss Craig, the lady from the agency, asked. "I want you to know, we also have therapists as part of our program. I know that this pregnancy is even more difficult for you. I can only suggest that you take advantage of our services and talk to someone."

She nodded, wiping at the tears she could no longer hold back. "I'm sorry," she managed to say. "I don't know if I can continue this today. I'm not changing my mind. It's just harder than I expected."

"I understand," Miss Craig said. "Clara, I'll be praying for you. And when you're ready, we will talk again. If you decide to use our agency, we'll have paperwork that needs to be signed."

"Okay," she said. Then she ended the call.

It had been too much, more than she'd realized, and she needed a friend.

She went in search of Tucker.

Tucker hadn't expected Clara to be in the living room. When he'd entered the house through the back door and heard her conversation, he'd poured himself a cup of coffee and headed for his office to take care of some bills that needed to be paid.

He started to sit down but he heard Clara moving. She'd left the living room and music came on in the kitchen. He left his office.

When he entered the kitchen the refrigerator door was open, and she was pulling out eggs, butter and milk. He watched from where he stood as she cracked eggs into a bowl and then poured a little milk in. She was beating the eggs with a fork when she noticed him.

"I'm making your breakfast. I felt the need to try again. After all, it is what you pay me to do."

"I pay you mostly because you have a way with Shay. She's happier since you came to work for us. She hasn't tried to scare you off. She doesn't get in trouble at school."

"She was just hurt and trying to get her mom's attention." Clara put a little butter in the skillet and turned the electric burner on.

Tucker closed the distance between them, taking a seat at the counter. "How'd it go?"

She blinked away tears and nodded, which wasn't really an answer. "What are you thinking?" she asked him.

"That I'm probably the last person you want to talk to. I don't have any answers."

"This is a lot harder than I thought it would be," she said, sharing more openly than she usually would. "It seemed like an easy decision, and then she talked to me about the type of people I want to choose to raise my baby. That's where I fell apart."

He got up and joined her on the other side of the counter. First, he turned off the stove because she'd already burnt the butter. She gave a watery laugh as he folded her in his arms and held her close, telling her it would be okay.

"What kind of parents do I want for my baby?" she asked as she leaned against his shoulder. "Real Christians. But how will I know if they're real or the kind of people who go to church once in a while? I want my baby to be loved and to grow up happy and healthy, raised with real faith."

"If you want to raise this baby, I'll help you. I'll be here for you."

She pulled back, looking up at him. "Tucker, that isn't…"

"Listen," he told her. "I'm not good at this. I'm not funny or charming or any of the things that you're probably looking for. But I'm a good man."

"You're the best of men," she told him. "And you deserve more than a woman in a predicament like this. I haven't thought about finding a father for this baby because I haven't thought about keeping it. From the beginning, I've thought only of the fear and pain I felt that night, and I just can't..."

"I know." He kissed the top of her head, her blond curls smelling of coconut. "Should you change your mind about keeping the baby, I'm here for you."

"That isn't what you want, Tucker. Not really. You're waiting for the right woman. There is someone out there who is meant to be yours, and if I let you do this, you'd regret it for the rest of your life."

His phone rang. He glanced down. "It's my sister."

"Then you should answer it," she told him, her hand rested on his cheek. He found himself regretting his hasty proposal that hadn't really sounded like one, anyway.

It hadn't been planned. It hadn't been wise. For a guy who didn't do impulsive, he'd done a lifetime of impulsive things in the past few weeks.

Even worse, he felt disappointed. He'd wanted her to say yes to him. Instead, she had gently let him off the hook, and as he answered the phone, she washed the pan and started over, determined to make him breakfast.

As he walked away, his sister's voice in his ear, he couldn't help but wonder if Clara Fisher might be The One.

Chapter Fourteen

Saturday afternoon Clara found Nan in her shop working on a boat. The process was slow, but Nan had always enjoyed it, piecing together the sanded wood and, in the end, giving customers something they would enjoy for years to come.

"You look fetching today," Nan said as Clara sat next to her, pulling up a chair and running her hand over the wooden Jon boat.

"Fetching?" Clara smiled at that. "Nan, we need to talk."

"My, this sounds serious." Nan sat back on her stool and gave her a curious look. "Is it about the baby?"

"A little bit, yes." Clara worried Nan wouldn't remember. Worse than that, she worried that if she went to Mexico, she'd be gone so long that when she came back, this woman who had loved her and helped raise her wouldn't remember her.

"Don't look so serious, chickadee. Christmas is only a week away. I know the holidays bring bad memories for you, but do something for me. Make new ones. Make new memories, and also focus on the good. We've had some good times, haven't we?"

"We have," Clara agreed as she reached for Nan's hand. "I'm going to Mexico for work. I'm leaving in a few days to go down and see the property I'll be working at. I won't be here for Christmas."

"Well, goodness, I didn't see that one coming. But what about the baby?"

Clara looked away. She knew she wouldn't be able to handle the expression on Nan's face when she told her. The hurt. The disappointment.

"Nan, I'm not keeping the baby. I've talked to an adoption agency."

"Oh, I see."

Clara looked at Nan and didn't see the emotions she'd thought she might see. Instead, she saw love and concern.

"I can't keep this baby, Nan." Clara's chest hurt with the memories of the night she'd been attacked. She took a deep breath and told Nan the story. Nan hugged her tight.

"I love you, honey, and there is nothing, absolutely nothing, too big for God. If this is the decision you've made, then God will help you see it through."

"Nan, what would I do without you?" Clara sniffled as she hugged her. "You're the best mom a girl could have."

"Now, you go calling me Mom and I'll have to give you the whole farm."

"I don't need the farm. I only need you."

Nan pulled back, a sweet smile on her face. "Honey, just pray about this decision to go to Mexico. I know it sounds like a dream come true. And I promise, if you go to work there, I'm coming to visit, but make sure it's right for you."

"I have been praying. And I'm counting on you visiting me there," Clara told her. "You can spend Christmases in Mexico with me."

"That's a deal. But don't run from your pain. Confront it head-on. If you run, it's going to keep chasing you. Pray. What if Mexico is your plan but God has something amazing for you right here in simple little Pleasant?"

"There is nothing simple about Pleasant," Clara assured her foster mom. "This will always be my home, but I'm a hotel manager, and I can't do that in Pleasant."

"No, you can't. Just be open to the fact that sometimes God has a different path."

"I'll be open, and I'll pray." Clara looked at her watch. "We have to go soon."

"Go where?" Nan asked in complete honesty. She'd forgotten.

"The Christmas Extravaganza," Clara reminded her.

The annual event brought people from all around the area. The town of Pleasant made Christmas come to life on the Saturday before Christmas. The buildings were decorated. Each church would have a special program they would perform in the community building on the main street. The stores, normally closed on Saturday evening, would be open for shopping. Vendors set up booths with crafts and food.

"Oh, yes, I'd forgotten." Nan said the last word on a breath that caught, but she quickly smiled. "We should get inside and get ready."

"We should. Nan, you are my mom. I want you to

know that. And I am so glad that God brought me to you."

"I'm glad, too. What would I have done without you girls?"

As they walked back to the house, Clara had to broach a subject that had been on her mind.

"Nan, would you like us to find Ryan for you?"

They walked in silence until they reached the back door of the house. Nan hesitated on the porch. "You know, I'm not really sure. He has never reached out to me, and he would be…" she closed her eyes "…he would be fifty-one."

"It's up to you," Clara said.

"I don't think so. Not yet."

An hour later they were walking through the double glass doors of the community building. From the sidewalk they'd heard a choir singing "O Little Town of Bethlehem."

"I do love this event, and I'm so glad they made it a tradition," Nan said as they walked to the back of the building where dressing rooms were set up.

They found Avery and Mrs. Wilson helping the children into costumes in one of the rooms. Shay and Quinn were dressed and helping smaller children slip into shepherd, angel and wise-man garb.

"How are you?" Clara asked Shay. Tonight she would sing her solo, and it was obvious from her jittery movements that she felt anxious.

"I'm nervous, but Avery said that she'd worry if I wasn't nervous. Nervousness is normal." Shay made a strained look. "I think I might throw up on stage."

"You won't!" Avery told the girl. "Deep breaths and

remember to focus on Nan. She'll be in the front row. I reserved a seat for her."

"Okay, got it. Eye contact with Nan." Shay gave Clara a searching look. "You'll be out there, too?"

"I will. My job here is done. I've helped get everyone dressed, and I'll be out front to help coach you all as you sing."

"It's *my* baby!" The plaintive cry drew their attention to Mary and Joseph. The two children were having a tug-of-war with the baby doll that would represent the infant Jesus. One of the shepherds jumped in and took the doll from the young parents. He shouted gleefully as he passed the doll to a wise man, but it was intercepted by Avery.

"That's enough," she said quietly.

The children quieted, and the baby doll was forgotten.

"Okay, I think Nan and I will leave you all, and we will go find our seats." Clara took her mother by the arm and led her down the hall to the open area where a stage had been set up.

Their reserved seats were empty, and Clara sat down next to Nan. As they waited for the show to start, Grayson and Tucker joined them.

"Now, isn't this nice," Nan said. "All of my kids, here together. I don't know where Regan is. I thought she said she'd be here."

"Regan doesn't live here anymore, Nan." Clara spoke softly.

"Now, don't go thinking there's something wrong with me every time I say something you don't know. Regan is coming home."

"Regan!" Clara was shocked. "You didn't tell us."

Nan made a face. "Well, I might have forgotten that part. But yes, she called. I don't remember when, but she's coming home."

The lights went out, and the program started. Nan clapped as the children came out onstage. Quinn stepped to the mic and began to read the Christmas story from the book of Luke. As she did, the children took their places. It was charming and sweet, and Shay's solo was the icing on the cake. As she sang, the star over the manger lit up. Then the three wise men journeyed to the stable, singing their song which was very comical. They made *wise*cracks and then they discovered the baby Jesus. Mary showed off the baby doll that had earlier been at the middle of the dispute. The shepherds came forward to bow before Him, one exclaiming that he was only a lowly shepherd and asking who would have thought he'd someday get to visit a king?

Shay stepped to the mic again, and all of the children stood and together they sang "Away in a Manger."

At the end, there was a standing ovation for the children. Nan clapped the loudest, and then she turned to Tucker and announced, "Did Clara tell you she's taking a job in Mexico?"

Clara wished the ground would swallow her up at that moment. Tucker had turned pale and silent. Before he had a chance to respond, they were suddenly joined by a couple Clara didn't know but who looked oddly familiar. The woman, in her midthirties, was tall and pretty and had light brown hair pulled up in a bun. The man greeted Tucker but then focused on Shay.

"Jana?" Tucker said.

Then Shay saw them. And she lit up like a Christmas tree.

But instead of running to her parents, she ran the other way. Tucker closed his eyes and sighed. When he opened them, Clara saw his anger, his pain and the concern he felt for Shay.

"Do you want me to go after her?" Clara offered.

He nodded.

Clara hurried backstage, hoping Shay hadn't escaped through a window or some such. Fortunately, she hadn't made it that far. She was in Avery's arms.

"They're probably here to tell me we'll never be a family again. I don't want to talk to them."

Avery held the girl in a tight embrace. "Look, Clara is here."

Shay turned, wiping at her eyes. "I don't want to talk to them."

"I think it would be good if you did." Clara held her arms out to the girl, and Shay hurried into her embrace. "I'll go with you."

Shay nodded. "But I'm not going with them," Shay whispered as they walked back down the hall to the auditorium.

"You're going to be okay," Clara reassured her, giving her hand a squeeze.

"Tell that to my stomach," Shay quipped.

Soon they were face-to-face with Jana and Kyle Bridges, and Clara watched as Shay stepped stiffly into her mother's arms. They would be okay, Clara told herself. Shay would always be loved and protected. Her gaze connected with Tucker's. He would protect his niece no matter what.

But would he forgive Clara for having learned about the job from Nan and not from her?

That was something she wouldn't know until later. At

the moment it seemed better to give Tucker, Shay and her parents the space and privacy needed. That meant walking away and leaving things unsaid.

As Tucker watched the surprise reunion between his sister and her daughter, he had a lot of feelings about Jana's unexpected arrival. She could have warned him, for one thing.

It felt a lot like this was about Jana's feelings and nothing at all about Shay's. He hoped he was wrong about that, but he couldn't help but be cynical, not after almost a year of raising his niece and having his sister claim she was just too busy with her career and that Kyle's job took him all over the world on business trips.

"We are trying to work things out," Jana told Shay first and then Tucker. "We want to make our marriage and our family work. I've been selfish. We've been selfish. You were right, Tucker. We were putting ourselves first. I'm so, so sorry, Shay."

Ignoring the apology, Shay told her mother, "I'm not coming home with you."

"But we want you to come home."

Shay shook her head, adamant. "No. I might come home, but not yet. I'm staying with Uncle Tucker and with Clara."

"Clara?" Jana gave Tucker a questioning look.

"The housekeeper," he answered. He would have to tell Shay that Clara was leaving soon. And he dreaded it, knowing his niece would suffer another blow at the loss of the woman who had become a good friend.

He was angry, but he reminded himself that Clara had always intended to leave.

"Let's go enjoy the festival," Jana told her daughter,

smiling as if she hadn't abandoned Shay and all was well. "We can talk later."

Tucker was unsure of what to say or do to help his niece. He'd never had to help his sister navigate these waters before.

"I'm not the same person I was when you left me here," Shay said with a maturity that Tucker realized had been developing for the past few months. "I've changed a lot, and I don't like the things I used to like. I go to church, and I have a horse. I have friends here. And family."

"We'll find a way to make this work," Kyle reassured his daughter. He looked like a broken man. Maybe a year without his wife or daughter had brought him some clarity.

The four of them left the building and walked down the sidewalk. The shops were decorated with Christmas lights, and Christmas music played from speakers that had been installed on light posts. The sights and smells of the season were all around them, and it should have been a festive occasion.

"Would you all like something to eat?" Tucker offered. "There's a booth up here with burgers and hot dogs, and another with smoked meats. The ribs are pretty good, too."

Shay made a beeline for the funnel cakes.

"I don't think that's real food," he called out, to no avail.

Jana Tucker took a step back and bumped into someone.

"Oof! Hey, watch it!"

He recognized that voice. "I'm sorry. I didn't know you were back there."

Clara gave him a sheepish grin. "I know. It's my fault. We weren't paying attention. We were heading for the funnel cakes."

"Tucker, would you mind if Kyle and I try to spend some time alone with Shay?" Jana glanced over at her daughter, giving him a hopeful look. "It was your message that brought us here. I listened to it a half dozen times, and then I called Kyle and told him we had to do something. I want a second chance with my daughter, and I know that it might take time."

"Go," Tucker told his sister. He wasn't feeling a lot of compassion for his sister, but he knew that Shay needed her mom. He had learned that from Clara.

"That leaves you free to join us," Nan told him as she took hold of his arm. "I'd like something to eat, and then I'm going back to the community building to watch the programs and music."

"I hear they have soup in bread bowls at the community building," Tucker told Nan as they carried on.

"That sounds wonderful," Nan said as she leaned heavily on his arm. Clara walked on Nan's other side and her foster mom slid her hand into hers.

Tucker had never thought of Nan getting older, getting frail. It was hard to accept, that this would happen to one of the hardest-working, most giving people he'd ever known.

As they entered the community center, Nan spotted a group of friends. She gave them a wave and then patted Tucker's arm.

"You two go on and have fun. I'll be right here with good friends and good food."

"You're sure?" Clara asked.

Nan gave her a quick hug. "More than sure. I have my phone. I can call if I need you."

"Would you like hot cocoa?" Tucker asked Clara as they left the center. "Maybe a corn dog?"

Clara walked next to him, obviously searching for an excuse for not having told him she was leaving. He told himself it was better this way. He'd always known she would leave. Better now than later. Right now he was just a little in love with her. In another month, he figured he'd be at the point of no return. It no longer mattered what he'd thought about relationships or what he thought he'd been looking for.

She'd changed it all. And now she'd probably break his heart.

"I know you're mad at me," she said as an upbeat a cappella group played over the speakers.

"Not mad," he told her. "Disappointed."

They walked on in silence.

They stopped at the corn dog vendor. He ordered two along with two hot cocoas. Others lined up behind them as they waited for their order. Tucker was relieved that no one he really knew had stepped in line. That meant no one trying to make small talk.

"When are you leaving for Mexico?" he finally asked as they walked away from the crowds, food in hand. They headed away from the Christmas festivities.

"Next week. I'll only be gone a few days. It's my dream job, the one I've always wanted. I'll be at a resort on the east coast. I'll have my own apartment on the resort property."

"You don't sound that excited," he noted.

"I am. It's a lot of change, but change can be good.

And I can't stay here. As much as I love it in Pleasant, there's nothing for me here."

"I think you're wrong. You have a lot of people in Pleasant who love you. People that are your family."

"I have good friends, too." She was looking up at him, seeming to include him on that list of friends.

"I do love being friend-zoned," he teased her.

"You know you're more than a friend to me," she assured him.

"Stay," he blurted out. "Don't leave. Please."

"I have to go. I have to get away." She tossed the rest of her corn dog into a trash barrel nearby. "I need somewhere to start over. I need something new. I'm going to have a baby, and after the baby is born, I'll give him or her to strangers. I'm going to need my work in order to keep my mind from dwelling on that decision."

"This could be your place to start over. I could be the person you start over with," he offered. He pulled off his cowboy hat and ran a hand through his hair. "That didn't come out right."

"Is that a proposal?" she asked, somewhere between shocked and teasing, as if she didn't know how to react.

"If it was a proposal, what would you say?" he asked.

She hesitated, and he wondered what she was thinking, but then she shook her head.

"I'd have to say no. You deserve someone better than me. You deserve someone you've known longer than a minute, someone you love, not someone you want to help."

"Someone better? I wish you believed in yourself as much as I believe in you."

"I've always struggled with that," she admitted. "It comes with the territory. Foster kid from an abusive home. I've worked very hard at believing in myself, but I'm not there yet. You deserve the truth, Tucker. The truth is I've always had a hard time believing that I can be loved. I spent years believing that even the God who created me couldn't possibly love me."

"Believe in yourself, Clara. If not me, then let someone else love you."

She put a hand to her belly and smiled softly, gently. When she looked up again, her eyes had filled with tears.

"You make me want to believe," she told him. "If I could ever believe in a happily-ever-after, I would want it to be with you. But you deserve everything, Tucker. And my life is too complicated right now. I'm still in recovery mode, trying to figure out the right next steps for myself and this baby."

"I know," he told her, hoping he didn't sound as if she'd just broken his heart.

He had to let her go. He'd known from the beginning that she wasn't for him. He just hadn't expected to want her to be his forever love.

Chapter Fifteen

Tucker sat in his dimly lit living room, the Christmas tree twinkling in the corner and a Christmas movie on TV. His sister sat across from him, looking as uncomfortable as he guessed she could get. Kyle looked a little less antsy as he sat next to his wife, holding her hand. They'd been in Pleasant for four days, playing the happy couple and courting their daughter, hoping she'd want to leave town with them.

He'd spent four days wishing he could get back to his life and not this—whatever *this* was. It had happened after the Christmas festival and Clara's announcement that she would be leaving. A yawning emptiness, a chasm of loneliness and obviously some dramatic feelings had taken over his life. He'd never been dramatic. But that's what broken hearts did to people, he supposed.

"We're really trying to make this work," Jana said, drawing him back to the present. She glanced uncomfortably around the room, then sighed.

"What do you want me to say?"

"That you forgive me?" she stated as she covered

her eyes with one hand. "I messed up. I did get self-ish. I hurt my daughter, lost a year of her life and also hurt my brother."

"I've been living my life just fine." Sort of. If that included maybe having his first adult broken heart.

Again, that might be a little dramatic. Hearts didn't really break. Also, men didn't suffer broken hearts. That was a thing reserved for women and romance novels, or so he'd always assumed.

"Are you listening to me?" Jana asked.

He shook his head. "Sorry, I wasn't. Did I miss something?"

"I asked if we could stay until school starts again in January." Jana scooted to the edge of the love seat. "She doesn't want to leave her friends just yet, she said. This will give her time to say goodbye."

He could imagine that pain, having their daughter tell them she wasn't ready to leave town and trust them with her happiness. He couldn't say that he blamed Shay. If he was being honest, he wasn't really looking forward to a silent, empty house. Shay had definitely brought life to the place.

So had Clara. But Clara had left for Mexico on Monday, having found a flight at a decent price. He didn't blame her, either. She had her reasons for wanting to start over. Leaving had always been her plan. He couldn't really say why it had taken him by surprise.

"Tucker, I know this is difficult…" Jana started.

He raised a hand to stop her. "It isn't difficult. Shay is always welcome here. And remember your promise to her. When she comes home, you go to church as a family. You eat as many meals together as possible. Also, you find a place for her horse to board." Suddenly, he stood up. "I have to go."

"Go?" Jana blinked a few times, and then her expression changed to one of sympathy and understanding. "Where are you going? Are you okay?"

"I'm fine. I just forgot I told Grayson that I'd look at a horse he has for sale today."

That hadn't been his plan, but as the words slipped out, it made sense. He needed fresh air and a horse. Grayson did have a horse Tucker had been thinking about buying. He might as well go to Grayson's. Actually, he wanted to go to Grayson's. A friend wasn't a bad thing to have at the moment.

When he pulled up to the house Grayson had built for Avery, he sat in his truck for a few minutes just thinking. He never thought he'd go down this path, but he kind of envied his friend. Grayson had a good life with his wife and daughter and probably a baby on the way. They had dinners together in the evening, church on Sunday. When they were together, they both looked happier than he'd ever seen them apart.

A pounding on his window made him jump. That was followed by him wanting to get out of his truck and pound on Grayson.

The truck door opened, and Grayson gave him a cheesy grin. "What's got you so worked up?"

"Not now," Tucker said as he climbed out, grabbing his hat as he did and shoving it down on his head.

"That's an expensive hat. Take it easy with the brim," Grayson said, stepping back and giving him space.

Probably a wise move on his part.

"I came to ride that roan of yours."

"I sold that horse last week. You said you didn't want

him." Grayson gave him another curious look. "You okay?"

"I'm fine." He really needed a ride. It was forty degrees, a little breezy, but the sky was blue. The kind of blue that only happens in winter. He wondered why the sky only had this depth of hue in the coldest months of the year.

"You miss her?" Grayson asked as they started toward the stable he'd built in the fall.

"The dark gold palomino? How could I miss a horse I've never seen?"

Grayson groaned at his attempt to change the subject. "Let me clarify. You miss Clara."

"Yeah," he admitted. He might as well be honest. "I miss her. Maybe I should try one of those dating apps like you suggested."

"I don't think that's the right thing to do."

"You're the one that told me to date," Tucker reminded him.

Grayson whistled shrilly, getting the attention of the horses that were grazing in the pasture. A bay, tall and leggy, raised his head. He had good coloring, a deep red-brown coat, a little shaggy from winter, but still a nice color. He had a black mane and tail. He wasn't the palomino, but he was a good-looking animal.

"Sure, I told you to date," Grayson said, once he had the horse's attention. "I didn't tell you to mess up and lose a good woman."

"You can't lose what you don't have," Tucker said as they entered the shadowy confines of the barn.

Grayson stepped into the feed room, pulled the light chain and filled a bucket with grain. On his way out, he grabbed a lead rope.

The horse was at the gate when they returned. Grayson handed over the lead rope. "Try him out."

"You didn't mention a bay." Tucker looked the animal over. Good size, probably sixteen hands, and nice conformation.

Grayson patted the horse's neck. "No, I didn't, but he's nice. You'll like him. And you're not going to have Clara if you don't do something to show her how you feel."

"If I was good at dating, I wouldn't still be single at my age."

Again, Grayson laughed. "Send her flowers. Say something that will get her attention."

"Flowers and words. I offered…"

Grayson looked a little stunned. "What? What did you offer?"

"Nothing." Tucker sighed. "I might have sorta proposed."

"Sorta?" Grayson sighed loudly. "You need a guide, some type of manual. If I'd known you were going to do something like that, I would have stopped you."

"Thinking back, I'm not sure if you're the expert on how to catch a woman," Tucker said. Grayson had left town years ago. He'd waited about twelve years to come home, and that's when he'd learned about his daughter Quinn.

"I think you should take my advice." Grayson returned to the original topic and ignored the reference to his own big mistake.

"Let's just talk about the horse. I want to be able to rope off of him and maybe take him to town for team roping." Tucker stopped and the horse stopped next to him.

"He's young, but I think you'd do okay with him," Grayson told him, pulling a saddle and saddle pad out of the tack room. "Saddle him up and try him."

The bay, named Chet, was skittish, but he could be handled. Tucker saddled the horse, then slipped the bridle over his head. The horse took the bit with no problem.

His phone rang. He ignored it for a few seconds, but then he pulled it out of his pocket. The horse sidestepped, unhappy with the outer space ringtone that Shay had put on his phone.

Tucker slid a hand down the horse's deep red neck. "Easy, boy."

"Are you talking to me?" asked a woman's voice on his phone.

He hadn't realized he'd answered. He looked down at the caller ID and almost hung up.

"Are you there, Tucker?" Clara asked, forcing him to answer.

"Yes, I'm here."

"Oh, good. I wanted to check on Shay. How's she doing?" Clara asked.

"She misses you," Tucker answered. He turned away from the bemused look on Grayson's face. He wasn't going to tell her that he missed her, too. Especially not in front of Grayson.

He missed her burnt scrambled eggs. He missed her singing along to the radio as she put away groceries and folded laundry. He missed watching her at the kitchen counter, head bent next to Shay's as they studied eighth-grade math. He missed having a cup of coffee with her in the morning.

He simply missed her.

"How are you doing?" he asked. "How's Mexico?"

"It's beautiful here," she answered. "I knew it would be."

He had so many questions. Was she happy? Had she talked to the adoption agency again? It had only been a few days since she'd been gone, not months or even weeks, so he doubted anything had changed. He let his questions go.

He had to let her go.

"Listen, I can't talk right now. I'm at Grayson's, looking at a horse."

"Oh, of course. I'm sorry. We'll catch up another time."

"Sure thing. We'll talk soon."

He couldn't make promises to be there for her. He couldn't make proposals that she wasn't interested in. She needed a new beginning in Mexico. He'd known all along that they weren't meant to be.

As soon as he hung up, the phone rang again. It was his sister.

"Tucker, we can't find Shay."

Clara stood at the edge of the water, the sand slipping away from beneath her feet as the waves washed in and out. Clear, turquoise water, soft white sand, an ocean breeze. She'd been a scared, hungry kid who had dreamed big. This was the fruition of those dreams.

She strolled back to the beach chair she'd abandoned and picked up the manila envelope that Avery had given to her. She had to tell the adoption agency the sex of the baby.

Okay, she could do this. She slid a finger under the flap and unsealed the envelope. Slowly, wishing she wasn't alone, wishing she didn't have to do this, she pulled out the ultrasound image.

Instantly her eyes filled with tears as she struggled to focus on the image of her baby. Hers. Not the baby of a man who had hurt her, left her bruised and broken. This baby moved inside her. It grew. Daily it became more and more a part of her.

She thought of the potential adoptive parents and wondered what they would name her baby. She wondered if they would take her child to concerts, show them the wonders of the ocean?

Out of nowhere, a soft, misty rain began to fall. The sky was no longer blue but heavy gray. She grabbed her beach bag and the envelope and walked back the way she'd come, back to the tiny house that was hers for as long as she stayed and managed this property.

Dreams do come true, she told herself as she entered the cottage with its pale yellow walls, white furnishings and large windows with views of the ocean.

She put the envelope on her desk, next to the sticky note reminding her to call the adoption agency. Her phone rang. She answered it, smiling when she heard Avery's voice.

"Hey, what's going on?" Clara asked casually.

"Clara, Shay is missing. She ran off yesterday afternoon. Tucker thinks she heard her parents talking about leaving in January."

"It's cold there, Avery," Clara pointed out.

"I know. I just thought you should know. There isn't anything you can do from Mexico, but you can pray. And maybe try to call her? Apparently she has her phone. Maybe if you call, she'll answer."

"Have they checked the app, the one that shows her location?"

"She's too smart for that. She turned it off. The police are trying to ping her phone, but the satellite signals for our area are pretty spotty."

"I'm so glad you called to let me know." She glanced out the window. The rain had already stopped, and the sun was peeking through the clouds. "What about Tucker? How is he?"

"Worried, but you know Tucker. He's staying busy searching for her."

"Tell him I'm praying. And I'll try calling Shay. If I get in touch with her, I'll let you know."

They talked for a few more minutes and ended the call. Clara walked to the window and prayed. She prayed for Shay, for her family. She prayed for her unborn child and the parents who would raise it.

Her phone dinged again. This time it was a text from one of her new coworkers, inviting her to join them for Christmas.

She hadn't thought too much about Christmas. It was only two days away, and the temperature would most likely hit eighty degrees here each day over the holiday weekend.

It would be strange to be here in this warm oasis, when at home people would be wearing warm coats, putting wood in the fireplace and drinking hot cocoa. Together. And she would be here, alone unless she accepted the invitation.

She put a hand to her belly.

"Well, it's just you and me. I hope someday you understand everything that we went through together. It isn't your fault, and I hope you know that." She wiped away a tear. "Grace."

She picked up her phone. First, she tried to call Shay, hoping and praying the girl would answer. The next few calls were made on impulse, and she questioned her sanity because it didn't make sense.

And yet, it did. It made sense because she'd been chasing a dream for a lifetime. But dreams could change. Plans could change.

Sometimes a person had to go out on a limb and do something a little bit different.

Chapter Sixteen

Clara waited six hours, then she made another call to Shay. No answer. She texted her, telling the teenager that they were worried and really needed her to answer so they could talk.

She prayed that the girl would respond. After all, tomorrow was Christmas. No one, not even Clara, wanted to be alone on Christmas.

Christmas was for being with people who loved you and that you loved, she thought, as she pulled the rental car up to Tucker's house. She was looking forward to being with the people she loved. At least for the next few days while she sorted out her thoughts and feelings and made sure Shay was safely home with her family.

Dudley greeted her as she got out of her car. The mastiff followed her to the front door. She knocked, waiting for Tucker to answer. It was his sister, Jana, who opened the door. The woman looked a wreck with tear-swollen eyes and her hair hanging loose and limp around her face.

"Clara," Jana said, surprise reflecting in hazel eyes so much like her brother's. "We didn't expect you."

"I should have called first," Clara said.

"No, it's fine. Come in, come in. I didn't mean it that way. I don't know what I mean anymore. Tucker isn't here. He's out searching. We've all been searching."

"No one has heard from her?"

Jana shook her head. "Not one word. No texts. No calls. Her friends all say they haven't heard from her."

Where would she hide if she was Shay? Clara followed Jana to the kitchen. They were sitting together, having a cup of tea, when Tucker walked in.

Tucker, tall and strong, but so tired and worn down that her instinct was to go to him, comfort him. He spotted her and froze.

"What are you doing here?" he asked, his voice hoarse from exhaustion.

"I came to help find Shay." She stood up, and without asking permission she wrapped him in a hug, wanting to give him the comfort he would have given her. "I'm here to help."

He drew in a breath and slowly exhaled, the gesture sounding rattled. His arms slowly crept around her, keeping her close as he kissed the top of her head.

After a minute he let her go. "I just came in to fill up my thermos, and then I'm going to try a few different places."

"I'll go with you," she offered.

"I don't know," he said, a wariness in his expression.

"Please, let me help find her."

He moved away from her and went to fill his thermos. When he finished, he closed it and nodded at her.

"Let's go." He looked to his sister. "Kyle and Grayson are searching some areas with abandoned homes. The sheriff has people looking in nearby caves."

Jana sobbed into her hand. "I can't believe this is happening. Tucker, what if someone took her? I'll never forgive myself."

"You have to stop thinking that way," Tucker said, trying to calm his sister. "Avery is on her way over here. She's going to sit with you for a while."

"Thank you." Jana hugged her brother tight. "I'm so sorry. For everything."

"I know."

They were on the road when an idea suddenly struck Clara. "Tucker, have you been to Nan's workshop?"

"Today?" He shot her a puzzled look. "Why?"

"Just a hunch. We should try looking there next."

They drove as quickly as possible to Nan's. Tucker pulled up to the workshop building, and they go out. Nan had stepped out on her back porch, and she called out to them, waving as they hurried into the space.

Once inside, Clara flipped on the lights and looked around. Nothing. No sound. No movement. But the room was warm, and she doubted Nan had been working in there.

Putting a finger to her lips to quiet Tucker, she led the way through the cavernous workshop to a room that few people knew about. Nan had a canning room that she used each fall to can her garden vegetables. The room had a stove, a fridge and food.

Clara pushed the door open, and they found Shay, wide-eyed.

"Shay!" Tucker rushed at his niece, pulling her into a hug. "What in the world were you thinking?"

Shay fought for a moment to get out of his embrace. Then she allowed her uncle to hold her. "I don't want to go."

"You don't want to go?" He held her away from him. "Do you think this is the way to solve a problem? Running away from the people who love you?"

"I don't know. I just didn't know what else to do."

Clara left them alone to talk things out. She walked back to the main room of the shop, her mind replaying Tucker's words to his niece. *Running away from the people who love you.* Wasn't that what she'd done? Yes, she'd taken a job that she'd always wanted. Her dream job. She'd taken the opportunity to start over where there wouldn't be nightmares chasing her at every corner.

But in reality, she'd also run away from her loved ones.

The door opened, and Nan rushed at her. "What in the world are you doing home?"

Clara hugged her foster mom. "I wanted to be with my family at Christmas. It seemed silly to spend it alone."

"Well, of course that is silly when you have people who love you."

"We found Shay," Clara told her foster mom just as Tucker walked out of the canning room with his niece.

"Well, Shay, what are you doing here?" Nan didn't seem at all surprised.

"Nan?" Clara said.

"Now, don't start looking at me like I've done something here." Nan shook a finger at Clara. "I'm as surprised as you are to see her."

Tucker was on the phone, his free arm around his niece as he talked to her parents. He continued to eye Clara, as if waiting for some big explanation. Or maybe he was wishing her gone again?

"I'm going to take Shay home to her mom," he said as he ended the call.

"I have to go with you," Clara reminded him. "My rental car is at your house."

"Right, of course." He released Shay long enough to hug Nan. "Sorry for barging in on you like this."

"I'm so thankful you found her. Shay, you gave us all a real fright, and I'm too old for that kind of scare."

Shay swiped at a tear. "I really am sorry."

"We know you are," Tucker said. "But being sorry doesn't make it okay."

Shay gave him a look, her nose wrinkled. "You sound just like a dad."

"Let's go." He led her to the door, not waiting for Clara.

Clara gave Nan another long hug. "I'll be home shortly."

"For good?" Nan asked.

"Just for Christmas," Clara answered.

Tucker had paused at the doorway, and when he heard her answer, he walked out, taking Shay with him.

As Tucker drove back to his place, he thought Shay and Clara were probably two of the most confusing ladies he knew. Shay had put them all through some torment for the past two days. And Clara was back in town, but for the life of him, he couldn't figure out why.

Best if he didn't try to figure either of them out.

He drove up to his place and had barely stopped the truck before Jana and Kyle had the door open and were hugging their daughter, promising her anything if she'd never scare them that way again.

"I don't want to go back to Jefferson City," Shay told

them. "I have friends here now. I have my church. And Uncle Tucker."

"But we're your parents, and we live in Jefferson City," Kyle told his daughter as they stepped into the house. "I know you love it here, but we love you, and we want to be a better family."

"Can't you just leave me here and visit?" Shay asked.

"No. We can't." Jana hugged her daughter close. "But we can come up with a compromise."

Clara stood at the door looking unsure. "I'm going to go," she said, her voice small and almost fragile.

Tucker took note of her tone and the look in her eyes. He shouldn't care. But he did. "I'll walk you to your car."

She drew him to her, no matter how hard he tried to pull away.

"I guess you'll be going back to Mexico as soon as Christmas is over?"

She hesitated. "I'm no longer sure what I'm doing, Tucker. When Avery told me that Shay was missing, all I knew was I had to come home. I had to be here for you. I'm glad I came, and I'm so glad that I thought of that room in Nan's workshop. She would have seen it when she visited."

"You mean when she tried to steal the moped."

They both laughed, and it felt good, like a release of the tension of the past couple of days.

"I looked at the picture," she said out of the blue.

"The picture?" He was a little lost.

"From the ultrasound that Avery did for me."

He felt his breath catch.

"It's a girl," she told him with a misty sheen of tears

in her eyes. "I didn't mean to, but I called her Grace. I didn't mean to name her."

"Oh, Clara." He hugged her. She was having a little girl. "No matter what, she'll be part of you. She'll have your features, your strength."

"But also, she'll be part his."

"The best of her will be you," he countered.

"I don't know what to do," she told him with all of that strength showing in her expression.

"You'll do the right thing."

"I wish I believed in myself as much as you believe in me." She fiddled with her car keys. "I have to let the adoption agency know that she's a girl."

"I see."

"I was supposed to make the call two days ago, and since I looked at the picture, I haven't. I needed time."

"And now?"

She nodded. "I'll make the right decision."

He wanted to give her options but interfering had never been his style. She needed to work through this on her own. He needed to let her.

He opened the car door for her. After all, his father had taught him to be a gentleman. He only wished his father had taught him how to avoid falling in love with a woman who seemed determined to run as far and as fast as she could from the people who loved her.

Clara and Nan were late for church on Christmas Eve. They entered the building as the choir sang "Silent Night."

A few people turned to see who the latecomers were. Nan waved to friends as Clara guided them toward the empty seats near Avery, Grayson and Quinn. It took a minute to find Tucker. She finally spotted him in the choir. He looked surprised to see her. He shouldn't have.

The music ended. Tucker and the other members of the choir left the stage to join their families. Pastor Wilson moved to the center of the stage.

"For unto you is born this day in the City of David," Pastor Wilson started. *"A savior, which is Christ the Lord.* A birth that not only was recorded for all of us to know, to read, to wonder over but that set in place historical events, even the way our years are numbered. We put up trees, we buy gifts, we sing carols and visit family, but truly, none of those things have to do with His birth. His birth is a celebration of our faith. Without it, we would have no faith. We could still put up a tree, string lights, buy gifts and visit family, but it was His birth that changed the world and can still change our lives in a very real way. Accepting His birth is the beginning of new life."

The sermon was short, and it was followed by another Christmas hymn. Clara closed her eyes and put a hand to her belly, feeling the sweet movement of her baby. She opened her eyes and when she looked up, she saw that Tucker was watching her.

A beautiful closing prayer ended the service. People moved from the pews, greeting friends and family, giving hugs and eventually moving toward the doors. Clara left her family and walked out of the church, looking up at the sky as she did. The brisk evening had turned dark and cold. The stars overhead were like diamonds in the velvety darkness. They were better than Christmas lights. They were so bright and appeared so close.

Tucker came to stand beside her. He also looked up at the inky black sky. "Amazing, isn't it?"

"It is. On a night like this, you can truly imagine the brilliance of a star and the wonder of those shepherds in a field."

"I think our families are giving us space. They believe we need to talk. Someone mentioned I should drive you home."

She smiled up at him, at the face that had become dearly familiar in the month that she'd known him. "Did they?"

"They did. If you look, you can see that they're all sneaking away without speaking to us. Avery told me to tell you we're meeting at Nan's for a late supper of sandwiches or leftovers."

"I'd like to walk," she told him. "I need some fresh air and peace before we enter that chaos."

"It's not too cold?" he asked, looking concerned.

"No, it isn't. Not for me," she teased. "Is it too cold for you?"

"Not at all." He reached for her hand.

As they put distance between themselves and the church, the sounds faded. Conversations and cars starting and leaving all became muted in the cold winter night.

"When do you go back to Mexico?" he asked.

They walked for a while, finding themselves at the bench near the creek. They sat down on the cold stone seat. She shivered and moved a little closer to his warmth.

"I'm not going back. It isn't the job for me. I'll find something else."

"Somewhere else?"

"Yes," she answered.

"Clara, tell me the truth. Why are you here?" Tucker touched her hand but didn't hold it. She missed him holding her hand. She'd missed him.

"I thought I could outrun my pregnancy," she told him. "I thought I could give the baby up for adoption and then live in Mexico, far from the memories."

"But you can't run from this."

"I know. I also don't want to run from it. It still hurts. I still have nightmares about that night. But I saw her face. I can't give her up."

She'd studied the picture looking for any resemblance to the man who had attacked her. Eventually the similarities would be there, but more than that, Clara would be there, too. "I feared I wouldn't be able to look at her. I thought I couldn't possibly love her. But even though she is part his, she is all mine."

"I'm glad you made this decision," he told her, looking at her with the sweetest smile on his face.

She had more to say, and she had to be brave.

"Tucker, I've spent my whole life running from my emotions. The other day I woke up in Mexico, in a dream cottage and in a dream job, and I realized it was no longer my dream."

"What is your dream?" he asked.

"You are." She stood up. "But I don't want a man who feels that marrying me would rescue me. I want a man who loves me and wants me in his life."

She waited to hear him say that he was that man. But he was silent.

So she gathered her strength and walked away.

* * *

Tucker stood there, in the place he'd been so many times in his life, the backyard of the church he'd grown up in. He'd stared at these same stars, wondered at this same night sky, and yet he had never felt this way before.

Clara's admission had left him speechless. He didn't know what to say or how to say what he felt. He let her walk away because he needed time to figure this out.

After a few minutes he followed her. He didn't chase after her. That would be desperate. Even though he was desperate to have her in his life, he didn't want to seem that way to the woman he planned on marrying.

Anyway, she couldn't leave: he had the keys to his truck.

When he caught up to her, she gave him an accusatory look. Obviously she didn't like that he hadn't answered her right away.

"You know I'm not impulsive, right?"

"I need you to be impulsive at this moment. I really need you to tell me if someone like you can love someone like me."

"Someone like you?" He put his arms around her. "Someone who's a survivor? Someone who's beautiful, kind and wise?"

"Tucker, the real me is a broken person who has had to learn how to survive," she told him. "Nan taught me to believe that I was more than a conqueror through Christ who gives me strength."

"You are strong and beautiful." He looked up at the sky. A shooting star raced through the darkness. "I was afraid of you. In the beginning I worried that I would fall in love with someone broken, someone who would break my heart. And then I realized that you're not broken. You've gone through difficult things, but you're still standing and stronger than anyone I know."

"I want to stay," she told him, her voice shaky, as if she feared his answer. "But I don't know how that looks for us. I don't know what I'll do. I don't have a plan."

"I want you to stay," he answered. "I want you to stay in Pleasant and stay in my life. We can figure out the plan later."

"I'm having a baby," she reminded him. "This baby, Tucker. After I was attacked and left broken and afraid."

"I know." He drew her closer. "I know."

"I'm keeping her. I'm keeping Grace." She said it out loud as if to remind herself that this was all real, and this was her plan.

"I would love you no matter what, Clara. I will also love your baby. I will love Grace."

"You're more than I ever imagined, Tucker. When I came home, I came here to heal and then move on with my life." She placed a hand on each of his cheeks, and he touched his lips to hers. The kiss, on that cold and starry Christmas night, changed everything.

They hadn't been looking for each other. They hadn't planned this. But God had known. He'd known they needed each other, and He'd known the love they would find when they stopped searching and allowed Him to bring them to this place.

They were meant to be.

He kissed her again, then took her to his truck and drove her home, to Nan's, to their family.

Epilogue

One Year Later

Pleasant Community Church was surrounded by snow on Christmas Eve. The evergreens next to the building were weighted down in layers of the heavy white stuff. It was as if God had decided to decorate for the occasion.

It did make the evening a little bit tricky. Sidewalks had to be shoveled, the parking lot had to be plowed, and cars drove a little more slowly. The guests were careful as they hurried up the sidewalk to the decorated front doors of the church.

Clara glanced out the window of the preschool classroom and watched as cars continued to pull into the parking lot. She hadn't expected people to show up, but she hadn't been able to cancel. They had the flowers, the cake, the food. Snow was an added benefit, even if she would be leaving it behind tomorrow, trading it for a beach in Mexico.

This time she wouldn't be going as a resort manager, she would be going as Mrs. Tucker Church. Clara

Church. The name made her giggle. She sounded like a church mouse in a children's book.

"What are you smiling about?" Nan asked. "You look so beautiful." For a moment Nan looked confused, but then she smiled, remembering. "Your dress is beautiful."

"I love it, Nan." Nan had always been an amazing seamstress, and when she had offered to make this dress, it had filled Clara's heart with joy. It was lovingly crafted with Nan's crocheted lace. It had taken months to make, and at times, Clara had tried to talk Nan out of the task. But Nan had insisted. As Clara looked at herself in the full-length mirror, she felt a bit overwhelmed by the gown. The soft fabric overlaid with the crocheted lace fell to the floor in soft waves, so fine and intricate.

"Nan, I love our dress." Clara hugged her foster mom. "And I love you."

"I love you, too, Clara." Nan brushed at her cheeks. "You girls are my joy."

"And you are ours." Clara took a deep breath, with no sign of Clyde the Elephant evident. He'd disappeared sometime in the past year, and she prayed he never returned. In his place she felt only peace. And hope.

"No tears." Avery, clad in a red velvet dress, hurried forward with makeup. "We have to keep our bride perfect."

Regan Ford, their foster sister who had returned to Pleasant in the summer, just shortly after Grace's birth, approached, holding the baby. Grace, now seven months old, was all giggles and sunshine. She wore a dress of soft lace to match her mommy.

Grace was everything wonderful. She was Clara's. She was also Tucker's. He loved Grace completely.

Today the three of them would become a family. They would make Tucker's house their home. They would share their lives together.

Quinn and Shay entered the room in their green Christmas gowns. They were junior bridesmaids, in addition to the flower girl, the ring bearer and the other attendants.

"The church is almost full," Shay informed them. "Tucker said no dallying. The weather might get worse."

"I would never dally." Clara pulled down her veil. Nan would walk her down the aisle. It seemed only right that she be the person to give the bride away. Nan, who had been both mother and father to her girls, teaching them to love God, love themselves and love life.

"Are you ready?" Nan asked.

"I'm very ready," Clara responded.

She and Nan followed the others from the room and down the hall. They walked out the side door into the snow, where men from the church waited with large golf umbrellas to protect them from the snow as they walked to the front doors of the church.

Avery met Grayson, the best man, and the two led the procession. Regan came next with Grace in her arms. Shay and Quinn followed.

The wedding march began to play, and Nan patted her hand, told her she loved her and that she would always remember this day. Clara couldn't stop the sob that broke loose.

"I love you, Nan. Mom."

"I love you, my girl."

As they walked down the aisle of the church, Clara

made eye contact with Tucker, the man who, from this day forward, would be her husband. Tall and imposing, he was a giant of a man in stature and in faith. He stood at the front of the church, unashamed of the tear that streaked down his cheek. He'd trimmed his curls and donned a tuxedo for this day.

She fell in love with him all over again.

Tucker had never considered himself a man who could be overwhelmed by his emotions, but today he was that man. His emotions for the woman walking down the aisle were immense. He gave a quick glance at his parents. They'd been home for a month, making the house in town their home again. They'd fully embraced his wife-to-be and her daughter.

He returned his attention to Clara, who stood before him now.

"Who gives this woman to this man?" Pastor Wilson asked.

"I do," Nan said, then she quickly hugged Clara, then Tucker. "Take care of my girl."

"Every day of my life," he promised.

Nan released him and went to take her seat by his parents.

He and Clara faced Pastor Wilson. On Clara's left, Grace began to giggle. She reached out to her mommy, struggling to free herself from Regan.

Tucker held up a hand to stop Pastor Wilson. "One second, Pastor."

He took Grace from Regan and held her close. She settled against his shoulder. His daughter.

"May I continue?" Pastor Wilson asked with a chuckle.

Tucker nodded.

The ceremony continued. Less than fifteen minutes later, they were united in holy matrimony, before God and their church. They were united as a couple, and as a family.

Tucker, Clara and Grace Church. As Tucker embraced both his wife and his daughter, he and Clara kissed beneath an arch of roses and mistletoe.

Life was good.

* * * * *

If you loved this story,
pick up these other books
from much-loved author Brenda Minton

Reunited with the Rancher
The Rancher's Christmas Match
Her Oklahoma Rancher
"His Christmas Family"
in Western Christmas Wishes
The Rancher's Holiday Hope
The Prodigal Cowboy
The Rancher's Holiday Arrangement
Her Small-Town Secret

Available now from Love Inspired!
Find more great reads at www.LoveInspired.com

Dear Reader,

When I began this story of Clara and Tucker, I had no idea where it would lead me as I thought of women who face situations where they feel lost, alone and judged. I wanted Clara to be a woman of faith, faced with a difficult decision while seeking answers through her faith. I wanted her to find joy, and also to find peace.

Then she found Tucker, a man who had his own ideas about how his life should look. Clara, he thought, would never be his future. In real life, when we make the declaration "never", we often close ourselves off from what God is trying to do in our lives.

I've said Never several times in my life. But God has a funny sense of humor. In answer to my never, God said, "Here are five children for you to love and raise." When I said "Never," God said, "No really, this is where I want you."

His will is always the very best place to be. It isn't always easy, but in His will and His presence, we find contentment.

Be kind and love one another. Remember that we all have a story, and we don't always know how it feels to live someone else's story.

Brenda

COMING NEXT MONTH FROM
Love Inspired Suspense

SEARCH AND DEFEND
K-9 Search and Rescue • by Heather Woodhaven

Undercover and tracking the assassin who killed his partner, FBI special agent Alex Driscoll accidentally pulls his partner's widow, Violet Sharp, and her search-and-rescue K-9, Teddy, into the case. Now, with Violet's life on the line, they have to work together to bring a killer to justice...and stay alive.

ROCKY MOUNTAIN STANDOFF
Justice Seekers • by Laura Scott

Someone will do anything to get federal judge Sidney Logan to throw a trial—even target her six-month-old foster daughter. And it's up to US Deputy Marshal Tanner Wilcox to keep Sidney and little Lilly safe. But with a possible mole in the courthouse, trusting anyone could prove lethal...

WILDERNESS HIDEOUT
Boulder Creek Ranch • by Hope White

Regaining consciousness in the Montana mountains with no memory of how she got there and an assailant after her, Dr. Brianna Wilkes must rely on a stranger for protection. But when hiding Brianna puts rancher Jacob Rush and his little girl in the crosshairs, they have to survive the wilderness *and* a killer.

TEXAS RANCH REFUGE
by Liz Shoaf

After cowboy Mac Dolan and his dog, Barnie, stop an attempted abduction, Mac is surprised to learn the target is Liv Calloway—the woman the FBI contracted him to investigate. Letting Liv hide from her pursuers on his ranch provides Mac the perfect cover. But is she a murderer...or a witness being framed?

COLORADO AMBUSH
by Amity Steffen

A mission to solve the mystery surrounding her sister's suspicious death sends Paige Bennett and her orphaned niece right into the path of ruthless gunmen. And jumping into Deputy Jesse McGrath's boat is the only reason they escape with their lives. But can Jesse help Paige uncover the truth... before it's too late?

BURIED COLD CASE SECRETS
by Sami A. Abrams

Searching for her best friend's remains could help forensic anthropologist Melanie Hutton regain her memories of when they were both kidnapped—and put her right back in the killer's sights. But can Detective Jason Cooper set the past aside to help her solve his sister's murder...and shield Melanie from the same fate?

LISCNM1221

Get 4 FREE REWARDS!

We'll send you 2 FREE Books plus 2 FREE Mystery Gifts.

Love Inspired books feature uplifting stories where faith helps guide you through life's challenges and discover the promise of a new beginning.

The Sheriff's Promise
RENEE RYAN

To Protect His Children
LINDA GOODNIGHT

FREE Value Over **$20**

YES! Please send me 2 FREE Love Inspired Romance novels and my 2 FREE mystery gifts (gifts are worth about $10 retail). After receiving them, if I don't wish to receive any more books, I can return the shipping statement marked "cancel." If I don't cancel, I will receive 6 brand-new novels every month and be billed just $5.24 each for the regular-print edition or $5.99 each for the larger-print edition in the U.S., or $5.74 each for the regular-print edition or $6.24 each for the larger-print edition in Canada. That's a savings of at least 13% off the cover price. It's quite a bargain! Shipping and handling is just 50¢ per book in the U.S. and $1.25 per book in Canada.* I understand that accepting the 2 free books and gifts places me under no obligation to buy anything. I can always return a shipment and cancel at any time. The free books and gifts are mine to keep no matter what I decide.

Choose one: ☐ **Love Inspired Romance Regular-Print** (105/305 IDN GNWC) ☐ **Love Inspired Romance Larger-Print** (122/322 IDN GNWC)

Name (please print)

Address   Apt. #

City   State/Province   Zip/Postal Code

Email: Please check this box ☐ if you would like to receive newsletters and promotional emails from Harlequin Enterprises ULC and its affiliates. You can unsubscribe anytime.

Mail to the Harlequin Reader Service:
IN U.S.A.: P.O. Box 1341, Buffalo, NY 14240-8531
IN CANADA: P.O. Box 603, Fort Erie, Ontario L2A 5X3

Want to try 2 free books from another series! Call 1-800-873-8635 or visit www.ReaderService.com.

*Terms and prices subject to change without notice. Prices do not include sales taxes, which will be charged (if applicable) based on your state or country of residence. Canadian residents will be charged applicable taxes. Offer not valid in Quebec. This offer is limited to one order per household. Books received may not be as shown. Not valid for current subscribers to Love Inspired Romance books. All orders subject to approval. Credit or debit balances in a customer's account(s) may be offset by any other outstanding balance owed by or to the customer. Please allow 4 to 6 weeks for delivery. Offer available while quantities last.

Your Privacy—Your information is being collected by Harlequin Enterprises ULC, operating as Harlequin Reader Service. For a complete summary of the information we collect, how we use this information and to whom it is disclosed, please visit our privacy notice located at corporate.harlequin.com/privacy-notice. From time to time we may also exchange your personal information with reputable third parties. If you wish to opt out of this sharing of your personal information, please visit readerservice.com/consumerschoice or call 1-800-873-8635. **Notice to California Residents**—Under California law, you have specific rights to control and access your data. For more information on these rights and how to exercise them, visit corporate.harlequin.com/california-privacy.   LIR21R2

"Are you okay?" Stone asked, tightening his hold around
her waist and gripping one of her hands.

"I— Yes." She didn't have time to explain to Stone
why this had nothing to do with her sore ankle, nor why
avalanches were her worst nightmare and that was the
real reason why she'd suddenly swayed in his arms.

Not when there was work to be done. There were
people in Holden Springs who needed help, and she knew
she should be there.

Tugger whined and pressed against her leg as he'd
been taught to do as a therapy dog. He could tell her heart
rate had increased and her pulse was pounding in her ears,
even if she didn't show it in her expression, although
there was probably that, too. The dog was responding to
cues most humans couldn't see, and Felicity reached out
and absently ran a hand between Tugger's ears to steady
her insides.

"Have they set up a temporary disaster shelter yet?"
she asked.

"Yes. At Holden High School," her sister said.
"They're using the cafeteria and the gym, I think. I'd go
myself except I have clients in the middle of service dog

back at the center. Do you mind taking Tugger
...ding out there?"

...city did mind. More than anyone would ever
...because she never talked about it, not even to her
...gs. But now was not the time to give in to those
...ngs. She could cry into her pillow later when she was
...e and the people of Holden Springs were safe.

"I'll take Tugger." She nodded. "And Dandy, too," she
...d, referring to a young black Labrador retriever who
...as part of the therapy dog program.

"I can tag along, if there's anything I can do to assist,"
Stone said. "That way you'll have an extra person for the
dogs."

Felicity was going to decline, but Ruby spoke up first.
"Thank you, Stone. They need all the help they can get.
From what I hear, there are a lot of families who were
suddenly evacuated from their homes."

"It's settled, then," Stone said. "I'm going with you."

Felicity didn't feel settled. The last thing she needed
was Stone alongside her. It would distract her from her
real work.

She sighed deeply.

A bruised ankle.

Stone's unnerving presence.

And now an avalanche.

Could things get any worse?

Don't miss
Their Unbreakable Bond *by Deb Kastner,*
available January 2022 wherever
Love Inspired books and ebooks are sold.

LoveInspired.com